Deputy Defender
CINDI MYERS

MILLS & BOON

First published in Great Britain 2018
by Mills & Boon, an imprint of HarperCollins*Publishers*
1 London Bridge Street, London, SE1 9GF

Large Print edition 2018

ISBN: 978-0-263-07894-7

MIX
Paper from
responsible sources
FSC® C007454

This book is produced from independently certified
FSC™ paper to ensure responsible forest management.
For more information visit www.harpercollins.co.uk/green.

Printed and bound in Great Britain
by CPI Group (UK) Ltd, Croydon, CR0 4YY

For Gaye

Chapter One

Yellow was such a cheerful color for a death threat. Brenda Stenson stared down at the note on the counter in front of her. Happy cartoon flowers danced across the bottom of the page, almost making the words written above in bold black ink into a joke.

Almost. But there was nothing funny about the message, written in all caps: BURN THAT BOOK OR YOU WILL DIE.

The cryptic message on the cheerful paper had been enclosed in a matching yellow envelope and taped to the front door of the Eagle Mountain History Museum. Brenda had spotted it when she arrived for work Monday morning, and had felt a surge of pleasure, thinking one of her friends had surprised her with an early birthday greeting. Her actual birthday was still another ten days away, but as her best friend, Lacy, had pointed out only two days ago, turning thirty was a milestone that deserved to be celebrated all month.

The message had been a surprise all right, but not a pleasant one. Reading it, Brenda felt confused at first, as if trying to make sense of something written in a foreign language or an old-fashioned, hard-to-read script. As the message began to sink in, nausea rose in her throat, and she held on to the edge of the counter, fighting dizziness. What kind of sick person would send something like this? And why? What had she ever done to hurt anybody, much less make them wish she were dead?

The string of sleigh bells attached to the museum's front door jangled as it opened and Lacy Milligan sauntered in. That was really the only way to describe the totally carefree, my-life-is-going-so-great attitude that imbued every movement of the pretty brunette. And why not? After three years of one bad break after another, Lacy had turned the corner. Now she was in school studying to be a teacher and engaged to a great guy—who also happened to be county sheriff. As her best friend, Brenda couldn't have been happier for her—and she wasn't about to do anything to upset Lacy's happiness. So she slid the threatening note off the counter and quickly folded it and inserted it back into the envelope, and dropped it into her purse.

"No classes today, so I thought I'd stop by and see what I could do to help," Lacy said. She hugged Brenda, then leaned back against the scarred wooden desk that was command central at the museum.

"I can always use the help," Brenda said. "But you're putting in so many hours here I'm starting to feel really guilty about not being able to pay you. If the fund-raising drive is successful, maybe there will be enough left over to hire at least part-time help."

"You already rented me the sweetest apartment in town," Lacy said. "You don't have to give me a job, too."

"I'll never find anyone else who's half as fun for that garage apartment," Brenda said. "At least if I could give you a job, I'd still be guaranteed to see you on a regular basis after you're married."

"You'll still see plenty of me," Lacy said. "But hey—I hear Eddie Carstairs is looking for a job."

Brenda made a face. "I seriously doubt an ex–law enforcement officer is going to want a part-time job at a small-town museum," she said.

"You're probably right," Lacy said. "Eddie certainly thinks highly of himself. He's been going around town telling everyone Travis fired him because he was jealous that Eddie got so much press for being a hero, almost dying in the line of duty and all." Her scowl said exactly what she thought of her fiancé's former subordinate. "Obviously that bullet he took didn't knock any sense into him. And as Travis told him when he fired him, Eddie wasn't on duty that day and he wasn't supposed to be messing around at a crime scene. And he wasn't a full deputy anyway—he was a reserve officer. Eddie always fails to mention that when he tells his tales of woe down at Moe's Pub."

"Is Travis as upset about this as you are?" Brenda asked. She had a hard time picturing their taciturn sheriff letting Eddie's tall tales get to him.

"He says we should just ignore Eddie, but it burns me up when that little worm tries to make himself out to be a hero." Lacy hoisted her small frame up to sit on the edge of the desk. "Travis is the one who risked his life saving me from Ian Barnes."

"And anyone who counts knows that," Brenda said. Ian Barnes—the man who had killed Brenda's husband three years before—had kidnapped Lacy and tried to kill her during the town's Pioneer Days celebration two months ago. Travis had risked his life to save her, killing Ian in the struggle.

"You're right," Lacy said. "And I'm sorry to be unloading on you this way. You've got bigger things to worry about." She glanced around the museum's front room, comprising the reception desk and a small bookstore and gift shop. Housed in a former miner's cottage, the museum featured eight rooms devoted to different aspects of local history. "How's the fund-raising going?"

"I've applied for some grants, and sent begging letters to pretty much every organization and influential person I can think of," Brenda said. "No response yet."

"What about the auction?" Lacy asked. "Are you getting any good donations for that?"

"I am. Come take a look." She led the way through a door to the workroom, where a row of folding tables was rapidly filling with donations people had contributed for a silent auction, all proceeds to benefit the struggling museum. "We've gotten everything from old mining tools to a gorgeous handmade quilt, and a lovely wooden writing desk that I think should bring in a couple hundred dollars."

"Wow." Lacy ran her hand over the quilt, which featured a repeating pattern of squares and triangles in shades of red and cream. "This ought to bring in a lot of bids. I might have to try for it myself."

"My goal is to make enough to keep the doors open and pay my salary until we can get a grant or two that will provide more substantial funds," Brenda said. "But what we really need is a major donor or two who will pledge to provide ongoing support. When Henry Hake disappeared, so did the quarterly donations he made to the museum. He was our biggest supporter."

"And here everybody thought old Henry was only interested in exploiting the town for his rich investors," Lacy said. "I wonder if we'll ever find out what happened to him. Travis won't say so, but I know since they found Henry's car in that ravine, they think he's probably dead."

Henry Hake was the public face of Hake Development and Eagle Mountain Resort, a mountaintop luxury development that had been stalled three and a half years ago when a local environmental group won an injunction to stop the project. Brenda's late husband, Andy, had been a new attorney, thrilled to win the lucrative job of representing Hake. But Hake's former bodyguard, Ian Barnes, had murdered Andy. Lacy, who had been Andy's administrative assistant, had been convicted of the murder. Only Travis's hard work had freed her and eventually cleared her name. But then Henry had disappeared. And only last month, a young couple had been murdered, presumably because they saw something they shouldn't have at the dormant development site. Travis's brother, Gage, a sheriff's deputy, had figured that one out and tracked down the couple's killers, but the murderers had died in a rockslide, after imprisoning Gage and schoolteacher Maya Renfro and her five-year-old niece in an underground bunker that contained a mysterious laboratory. A multitude of law enforcement agencies was still trying to untangle the goings-on at the resort—and no one seemed to know what had happened to Henry Hake or what the young couple might have seen that led to their murders.

"I guess I don't understand how these things work," Lacy said. "But it doesn't seem very smart to base a budget on the contributions of one person. What if Henry had suddenly decided to stop sending checks?"

"Henry's contributions were significant,

but they weren't all our budget," Brenda said. "When I started here four years ago, we had a comfortable financial cushion that generated enough income for most of our operating expenses, but that's gone now." Her stomach hurt just thinking about it.

"Where did it go?" Lacy asked. But the pained expression on Brenda's face must have told her the truth. "Jan!" She hopped off the desk. "She siphoned off the money to pay the blackmail!" She put her hand over her mouth, as if she wished she could take back the words. "I'm so sorry, Brenda."

Brenda had learned only recently that before his death, Andy had been blackmailing her former boss, Eagle Mountain mayor Jan Selkirk, over her affair with Henry Hake. "It's all right," she said. "I can't prove that's what happened, but probably. But if that is what happened, I don't know where the money went. I mean, yeah, Andy used some of it for the improvements on our house, and to buy some stuff, but not the tens of thousands of dollars we're talking about."

"Maybe Jan was giving the money to Henry, and his donations were his guilty conscience forcing him to pay you back," Lacy said.

"That would fit this whole sick soap opera, wouldn't it?" Brenda picked up a battered miner's lantern and pretended to examine it.

Lacy rubbed Brenda's shoulder. "None of this is your fault," she said. "And you're doing an amazing job keeping the museum going. These auction items should pull in a lot of money. Didn't you tell me that book you found is worth a lot?"

The book. A shudder went through Brenda at the thought of the slim blue volume she had found while going through Andy's things a few weeks ago. *The Secret History of Rayford County, Colorado.* What had at first appeared to be a run-of-the-mill self-published local history had turned out to be a rare account of a top-secret government program to produce biological weapons in the remote mountains of Colorado during World War II. Was that what had whoever left the threatening note so upset? Did they object to the government's dirty secrets being aired—even though the operation had ended seventy years ago?

In any case, Brenda's online research had revealed an avid group of collectors who were anxious to get their hands on the volume, and willing to pay for the privilege. Thus was born the idea of an auction to fund the museum—and her salary—for the immediate future.

"I still can't imagine what Andy was doing with a book like that," she said. "But I guess it's obvious I didn't know my husband as well as I thought."

"Whyever he had it, I'm glad it's going to help you now," Lacy said.

The local paper had run an article about the fund-raiser, and listed the book among the many donations received. That must be where the letter writer had found out about it. Was it just some crank out to frighten her? Could she really take seriously a letter written on yellow stationery with cartoon flowers?

But could she really afford not to take it seriously? She needed to let someone else know about the threat—someone with the power to do something about it. "Can you do me a favor and watch the museum for a bit?" Brenda asked.

"Sure." Lacy looked surprised. "What's up?"

"I just have an errand I need to run." She retrieved her purse from beneath the front counter and slung it over her shoulder. "It shouldn't take more than an hour." She'd have to ask the sheriff to keep the letter a secret from his fiancée, at least for now. In fact, Brenda didn't want anyone in town to know about it. She had been the focus of enough gossip since Andy's murder. But she wasn't stupid enough to try to deal with this by herself. She figured she could trust the Rayford County

Sheriff's Department to keep her secret and, she hoped, to help her.

DEPUTY DWIGHT PRENTICE would rather face down an irate motorist or break up a bar fight than deal with the stack of forms and reports in his inbox. But duty—and the occasional nagging from office manager Adelaide Kincaid—forced him to tackle the paperwork. That didn't stop him from resenting the task that kept him behind his desk when Indian summer offered up one of the last shirtsleeve days of fall, the whole world outside bathed in a soft golden light that made the white LED glare of his office seem like a special kind of torture.

As he put the finishing touches on yet another report, he wished for an urgent call he would have to respond to—or at least some kind of distraction. So when the buzzer sounded that signaled the front door opening, he sat back in his chair and listened.

"I need to speak with Travis."

The woman's soft, familiar voice made Dwight slide back his chair, then glance at the window to his left to check that the persistent cowlick in his hair wasn't standing up in back.

"Sheriff Walker is away at training." Adelaide spoke in what Dwight thought of as her schoolmarm voice—very precise and a little chiding.

"Could I speak to one of the deputies, then?"

"What is this about?"

"I'd prefer to discuss that with the deputy."

Dwight rose and hurried to head off Adelaide's further attempts to determine the woman's business at the sheriff's department. The older woman was a first-class administrator, but also known as one of the biggest gossips in town.

"Hello, Brenda." Dwight stepped into the small reception area and nodded to the pretty blonde in front of Adelaide's desk. "Can I help you with something?"

"Mrs. Stenson wants to speak to a deputy," Adelaide said.

"That would be me." Dwight indicated the hallway he had just moved down. "Why don't you come into my office?"

As he escorted her down the hall, Dwight checked her out, without being too obvious. Brenda had been a pretty girl when they knew each other in high school, but she had matured into a beautiful woman. She had cut a few inches off her hair recently and styled it in soft layers. The look was more sophisticated and suited her. He had noticed her smiling more lately, too. Maybe she was finally getting past the grief for her murdered husband.

She wasn't smiling now, however. In his office, she took a seat in the chair Dwight indicated and he shut the door, then slid behind his desk. "You look upset," he said. "What's happened?"

In answer, she opened her purse, took out a

bright yellow envelope, and slid it across the desk to him.

He looked down at the envelope. BRENDA was written across the front in bold black letters, all caps. "Before I open it, tell me your impression of what's in it," he said.

"I don't know if it's some kind of sick joke, or what," she said, staring at the envelope as if it were a coiled snake. "But I think it might be a threat." She knotted her hands on the edge of the desk. "My fingerprints are probably all over it. I wasn't thinking..."

"That's all right." Dwight opened the top desk drawer and took out a pair of nitrile gloves and put them on. Then he turned the envelope over, lifted the flap and slid out the single sheet of folded paper.

The capital letters of the message on the paper were drawn with the same bold black marker as the writing on the envelope. BURN THAT BOOK OR YOU WILL DIE.

"What book?" he asked.

"I can't be sure, but I think whoever wrote that note is referring to the rare book that's part of the auction to raise funds for the museum. It's an obscure, self-published volume purportedly giving an insider's experiences with a top-secret project to manufacture biological weapons for use in World War II. The project was apparently financed by the US government and took place in Rayford County. I found it in Andy's belongings, mixed in with some historical law books. I have no idea how he came to have it, but apparently it's an item that's really prized by some collectors—because it's rare, I guess. And maybe because of the nature of the subject matter."

Dwight grabbed a legal pad and began making notes. Later, he would review them. And he would need them for the inevitable report. "Who knew about this book?" he asked.

"Lots of people," she said. "There was an article in the *Examiner*."

"The issue that came out Thursday?"

She nodded. "Yes."

He riffled through a stack of documents on his desk until he found the copy of the newspaper. The article was on the front page. Rare Book to Head Up Auction Items to Benefit Museum—accompanied by a picture of Brenda holding a slim blue volume, the title, *The Secret History of Rayford County, Colorado*, in silver lettering on the front. "How much is the book worth?" he asked.

"A dealer I contacted estimated we could expect to receive thirty to fifty thousand dollars at a well-advertised auction," she said. "I thought that in addition to the money, the auction would generate a lot of publicity for the museum and maybe attract more donors."

"People will pay that much money for a book?" Dwight didn't try to hide his amazement.

"I was shocked, too. But apparently, it's very rare, and there's the whole top-secret government plot angle that collectors like."

"But this note wasn't written by a collector," he said. "A collector wouldn't want you to burn the book."

"I know." She leaned toward him. "That's why I'm wondering if the whole thing is some kind of twisted joke. I mean—that cheerful yellow paper..." Her voice trailed away as they both stared at the note.

"Maybe it's a joke," he said. "But we can't assume anything. Has anyone said anything to you about the book since this article ran?" He tapped the newspaper. "Anything that struck you as odd or 'off'?"

"No. The only thing anyone has said is they hope we get a lot of money for the museum. A couple of people said they couldn't imagine who would pay so much for a book, and one or two have said the subject matter sounded interesting. But no one has seemed upset or negative about it at all."

"Where is the book now?" he asked.

"It's at the museum."

The old-house-turned-museum wasn't the most secure property, from what Dwight could remember about it. "Do you have a security system there—alarms, cameras?"

She shook her head. "We've never had the budget for that kind of thing. And we've never needed it. We just have regular door locks with dead bolts, and we keep the most valuable items in our collection in locked cases. But we don't really have much that most people would find valuable. I mean, antiques and historical artifacts aren't the kind of thing a person could easily sell for quick cash."

"But this book is different," Dwight said. "It's worth a lot of money. I think you had better put it somewhere else for now. Somewhere more secure."

"I was thinking of moving it to a safe at my house."

"That sounds like a good idea." He stood. "Let's go do that now."

"Oh." She rose, clearly flustered. "You don't have to do that. I can—"

"I'd like to see this book, anyway." He gestured to the door, and she moved toward it.

"I'll meet you at the museum," he said when they reached the parking lot.

She nodded and fished her car keys out of her purse, then looked at him again, fear in her hazel eyes, though he could tell she was trying hard to hide it. "Do you think I'm really in danger?" she asked.

He put a hand on her arm, a brief gesture of reassurance. "Maybe not. But there's no harm in being extra careful."

She nodded, then moved to her car. He waited until she was in the driver's seat before he got into his SUV, suppressing the urge to call her back, to insist that she ride with him and not move out of his sight until he had tracked down the person who threatened her. He slid behind the wheel and blew out his breath. This was going to be a tough one—

not because they had so little to go on to track down the person who had made the threat, but because he was going to have to work hard to keep his emotions out of the case.

He started the vehicle and pulled out onto the street behind Brenda's Subaru. He could do this. He could investigate the case and protect Brenda Stenson without her finding out he'd been hopelessly in love with her since they were both seventeen.

Chapter Two

Brenda had come so close to asking Dwight if he would drive her to the history museum in the sheriff's department SUV. She felt too vulnerable in her own car, aware that the person who wrote that awful note might be watching her, maybe even waiting to make good on his threat. She shuddered and pushed the thought away. She was overreacting. Dwight hadn't seemed that upset about the note. And really, who could take it seriously, with the yellow paper and cartoon flowers?

She had always admired Dwight's steadiness. When they had been in high school, he was one of the stars on the basketball team. As a cheerleader, she had attended every game and watched him lope up and down the gym on his long legs. She had watched all the players, of course, but especially him. He had thick chestnut hair and eyes the color of the Colorado sky in a ruggedly handsome face. There was something so steady about him, even then. Like many of her classmates, he was the son of a local rancher. He wore jeans and boots and Western shirts and walked with the swaggering gait that came from spending so much time on horseback.

A town girl, she didn't have much in common with him, and was too shy to do more than smile at him in the hall. He always returned the greeting, but that was as far as it went. He'd never asked her out, and after graduation, they'd both left for college. She had returned to town five years later as a newlywed, her husband, Andy, anxious to set up his practice in the small town he had fallen in love with on visits to meet her family. Dwight returned a year later, fresh from military service in Afghanistan. Brenda would have predicted he would go to work on the family ranch—the choice of law enforcement surprised her. But the job suited him—the steadiness and thoughtfulness she had glimpsed as a teen made him a good cop. One she was depending on to help her through this latest crisis.

When they entered the history museum, Lacy was talking to a wiry young man with buzzed hair and tattoos covering both forearms. "Brenda!" Lacy greeted them, then her eyebrows rose as Dwight stepped in behind her. "And Dwight. Hello." She turned to the young man. "Brenda is the person you need to talk to."

"Hello, Parker," Dwight said.

"Deputy." The young man nodded, his expression guarded.

"This is Parker Riddell," Lacy said. "Paige

Riddell's brother. Parker, this is Brenda Stenson, the museum's director."

Paige ran the local bed-and-breakfast and headed up the environmental group that had stopped Henry Hake's development. Brenda couldn't recall her ever mentioning a brother. "It's nice to meet you," she said, offering her hand. "How can I help you?"

Parker hesitated, then took it. "I was wanting to volunteer here," he said.

"Are you interested in history?" Brenda asked.

"Yeah. And my sister said you could use some help, so…" He shrugged.

"Well, yes. I can always use help. But now isn't really a good time. Could you come back tomorrow?"

"I guess so." Parker cut his eyes to Dwight. "Is something wrong?"

"No. Deputy Prentice is here to discuss security for our auction." Brenda forced a smile. That sounded like a reasonable explanation for

Dwight's presence, didn't it? And not that far from the truth.

"Okay, I guess I'll come back tomorrow." Keeping his gaze on Dwight, he sidled past and left, the doorbells clanging behind him.

"What was that about?" Lacy asked Dwight. "He was looking at you like you were a snake he was afraid would strike—or a bug he wanted to stomp on."

"Let's just say Parker has a rocky history with law enforcement. I'd be careful about taking him on as a volunteer."

He sounded so serious. "Do you think he's dangerous?" Brenda asked.

Dwight shifted his weight. "I just think he's someone who should be watched closely."

"I'll keep that in mind." Brenda turned to Lacy. "Thanks for looking after things here while I was gone. You can go home now. I'm going to go over some things with Dwight, then close up for lunch."

Lacy gave her a speculative look, but said

nothing. "We'll talk later," she said, then collected her purse and left.

Brenda crossed her arms and faced Dwight. "What's the story on Parker Riddell?" she asked.

He rubbed the back of his neck. "I probably shouldn't tell you."

"This is a very small town—you know I'll find out eventually. If anyone links the information back to you, you can tell them I was doing a background check prior to taking him on as a volunteer. That's not unreasonable."

"All right." He leaned back against the counter facing her. "He got into trouble with drugs, got popped for some petty theft, then a burglary charge. He did a little jail time, then went into rehab and had a chance at a deferred sentence."

"What does that mean?" she asked.

"It means if he keeps his nose clean, his record will be expunged. I take it he came to live with Paige after he got out of rehab to get away from old friends and, hopefully, bad habits. And I hope he does that. That doesn't mean I think it's the best idea in the world for you to spend time alone with him, or leave him alone with anything around here that's valuable."

"Do you think he might have sent the note?"

He frowned. "It doesn't fit any pattern of behavior he's shown before—at least that I know of. But I can look into it. I *will* look into it."

"I can't think of anyone who would do something like that," she said. "I mean, anonymous notes—it's so, well, sleazy. And over a stupid book."

"Show me the book."

"It's back here." She led the way into the workroom, to a file drawer in the back corner. She had placed *The Secret History of Rayford County, Colorado* inside an acid-free cardboard box. She opened the box and handed the book to Dwight.

He read the title on the front, then opened

it and flipped through it, stopped and read a few lines. "It's a little dry," he said.

"Some parts are better than others," she said. "Collectors are mainly interested because of the subject matter and its rarity."

He returned the book to her. "Maybe someone is upset that this top-secret information has been leaked," he said.

"The whole thing happened seventy years ago," she said. "As far as I can determine, most of the details about the project are declassified, and all the people who took part are long dead."

"A relative who's especially touchy about the family name?" Dwight speculated. "Someone related to the author?" He examined the spine of the book. "S. Smith."

"The research I did indicated the name is probably a pseudonym," Brenda said. "In any case, since the author was supposedly part of the project, he would most likely be dead by now. Since his real identity has never been made public, what is there for the family to be upset about?"

"Someone else, then," Dwight said.

"Are there any new suspicious people hanging around town?" she asked.

He shook his head. "No one who stands out."

"Except Parker," she said.

"I'll check into his background a little more, see if I can find a connection," he said. He turned to survey the long table that took up much of the room. "Are these the items for the auction?"

"Everything I've collected so far," she said. "I still have a few more things people have promised."

He picked up a set of hand-braided reins and a silver-trimmed bridle. "You've got a lot of nice things. Should net you a good bit of money."

"I hope it's enough," she said. "I don't suppose you have any hope of finding Henry Hake alive and well and enjoying an island vacation, have you? He was our biggest donor."

Dwight shook his head. "I don't expect any of us will be seeing Henry Hake again," he said. "At least not alive."

"I figured as much. So all we need is another wealthy benefactor. I'm hoping that rare book will attract someone like that—someone with money to spare, who might enjoy getting credit for pulling us out of the red."

"What will happen if that benefactor doesn't materialize?" he asked.

She straightened her shoulders and put on her brave face—one she had had plenty of practice assuming since Andy's death. "I'll have to find another job. And this town will lose one of its real assets."

"I hope we won't lose you, too," he said.

The intensity of his gaze unsettled her. She looked away. "Sometimes I think leaving and starting over would be a good idea," she said.

"But I love Eagle Mountain. This is my home, and I'm not too anxious to find another one."

"Then I hope you never have to."

The silence stretched between them. She could feel his eyes still on her. Time to change the subject. "Lacy was telling me Eddie Carstairs has been mouthing off to people about his getting fired, trying to stir up trouble."

"Eddie's sore about losing his job, but Travis did the right thing, firing him. Any other department would have done the same. The fact that he's making such a fuss about something that was his own fault shows he doesn't have the right temperament for the job. You can't be hotheaded and impulsive and last long in law enforcement."

Dwight had never been hotheaded or impulsive. He was the epitome of the cool, deliberate, hardworking cowboy. She replaced the book in the box and fit the lid on it. "I don't want to keep you any longer. I'll close a little early for lunch and you can follow me to the house—though that probably isn't necessary."

"No harm in taking precautions." He followed her into the front room, where she collected her purse, turned down the lights, then turned the sign on the front door to Closed. "After we secure the book in your safe, maybe I could take you to lunch," he said.

The invitation surprised her so much she almost dropped the book. Was Dwight asking her out on a *date*? *You're not in high school anymore*, she reminded herself. He was probably just being friendly. Her first instinct was to turn him down. She had too much to do. She wasn't ready to go out with another man.

Andy's been dead three and a half years. When are *you going to be ready?*

"Thanks," she said. "That would be nice."

He walked her to her car, and when his arm brushed hers briefly as he reached out to open the door for her, a tremor went through her. Why was she acting like this? She wasn't a schoolgirl anymore, swooning over a crush—but that's what being with Dwight made her feel like all of a sudden.

She murmured, "Thanks," as she slid past him into the driver's seat and drove, sedately, toward her home. She laughed at herself, being so careful to keep under the speed limit. Did she really think Dwight would suddenly switch on his lights and siren and give her a ticket?

The house she and Andy had purchased when they moved back to Eagle Mountain had undergone extensive remodeling, expanding from a tiny clapboard-sided bungalow to a larger cottage trimmed in native rock and including a detached two-car garage with an apartment above. Only recently, Brenda had learned that those renovations had been financed not by Andy's law practice, as she had thought, but with money he received from people he blackmailed, including her former boss, Jan Selkirk. The knowledge had made her feel so ashamed, but people had been surprisingly kind. No one had suggested—at least to her face—that she had been guilty of anything except being naive about her husband's activities.

She pulled into the driveway that ran between the house and the garage and Dwight parked the sheriff's department SUV behind her. That would no doubt raise some eyebrows among any neighbors who might be watching. Then again, considering all that had happened in the past three and a half years, from Andy's murder to the revelations about his blackmail and Jan's attempts to steal back evidence of her involvement in the blackmail, everyone in town was probably used to seeing the cops at Brenda's place.

Dwight met her on the walkway that led from the drive to the front steps. "You haven't had any trouble around the house, have you?" he asked. "No mysterious phone calls or cars you don't recognize driving by? Any door-to-door salesmen who might have been casing the place?"

"If door-to-door salesmen still exist, they aren't in Eagle Mountain." She led the way up the walk, keys in hand.

He smiled at her, and her heart skipped a beat again. He really did have the nicest smile, and those blue, blue eyes—

The eyes hardened, and the smile vanished. She realized he wasn't focused on her anymore, but on her front door. She gasped when she saw the envelope taped there—a bright yellow envelope. Like a birthday card, but she was pretty sure it wasn't. Her name, printed in familiar bold black lettering, was written on the front.

Dwight put his hand on her shoulder. "Wait before you touch it. I want to get some photographs."

He took several pictures of the note taped to the door, from several different angles, then moved back to examine the steps and the porch floor for any impressions. He put away his phone and pulled on a pair of thin gloves, then carefully removed the note from the door, handling it by the edges and with all the delicacy one would use with a bomb.

Meanwhile, Brenda hugged her arms across her stomach and did her best not to be sick in the lilac bushes. Dwight laid the envelope on the small table beside the porch glider and teased open the flap.

The note inside was very like the first— yellow paper, dancing cartoon flowers. He coaxed out the sheet and unfolded it. Brenda covered her mouth with her hand. Taped to the top of the paper was a photograph—a crime scene photo taken of Andy at his desk, stabbed in the chest, head lolling forward. Brenda squeezed her eyes shut, but not before she had seen the words written below the photograph. THIS COULD BE YOU.

Chapter Three

Dwight could feel Brenda trembling and rushed to put his arm around her and guide her over to a cushioned lounge chair on the other side of the porch, away from the sick photo. He sat beside her, his arm around her, as she continued to shudder. "Take a deep breath," he said. "You're safe."

She nodded, and gradually the trembling subsided. Her eyes met his, wet with unshed tears. "Why?" she whispered.

"I don't know. I'm going to look at the note again. Will you be okay if I do that?"

"Yes." She straightened. "I'm fine now. It

was just such a shock." She was still pale, but determination straightened her shoulders, and he didn't think she would faint or go into hysterics if he left her side.

He stood and returned to the note on the table. The image pasted onto the paper wasn't a photograph, but a photocopy of a photograph. Dwight couldn't be sure, but this didn't look like something that would have run in the newspaper. It looked like a crime scene photo, the kind that would have been taken before Andy Stenson's body was removed from his office and then become part of the case file.

"Have you ever seen this photograph before?" he asked Brenda.

"I think so," she said. "At Lacy's trial."

Dwight nodded. Lacy Milligan had been wrongfully convicted of murdering her boss. At the trial, the prosecution would have shown crime scene photos as evidence of the violence of the attack.

"Who would have had access to those photos?" Brenda asked. "Law enforcement, the lawyers—"

"Anyone who worked at the law offices or the courtroom," Dwight said. "Maybe even the press. This isn't one of the actual photos—it's a photocopy. The person who wrote the note included it to frighten you."

"Well, they succeeded." She stood and began pacing back and forth, keeping to the side of the porch away from the note and its chilling contents. "Dwight, what are we going to do?"

He liked that "we." She was counting on him to work with her—to help her. "You could burn the book," he said.

She stopped pacing and stared at him. "And give in to this creep's demands? What's to stop him from demanding something else? Maybe next time he'll suggest I burn down my house, or paint the museum pink. Maybe he gets off on making people do his bidding." Her voice rose, and her words grew more agitated—but it was better than seeing her so pale and de-feated-looking.

"I'm not saying you should burn the book, only that it was one option."

"I'm not going to burn the book. We need to find out who this person is and stop him—or her."

She was interrupted by a red car pulling to the curb in front of the house. Lacy got out and hurried up the walk, smiling widely. "Hey, Dwight," she said. "Still discussing security issues?" She laughed, then winked at Brenda.

Brenda's cheeks flushed a pretty pink. "You're certainly in a good mood," she said.

"I've been out at the ranch. The wedding planner needed me to take some measure-ments. It's such a gorgeous place for a wed-ding, and Travis's mom is as excited about it as I am." She sat in a chair near Brenda. "So what are you two really up to?" she asked.

"I've received a couple of disturbing letters,"

Brenda said. She glanced at Dwight. "Threatening ones."

"Oh no!" Lacy's smile vanished and her face paled. "I thought you were a little distracted this morning, but I assumed it was over the auction. I'm sorry for being so silly."

"It's all right," Brenda said. "The first note was taped to the door of the museum when I arrived this morning. We just found a second one here at the house."

"Threats?" Lacy shook her head. "Who would want to threaten you? And why?"

"The first note told me I should burn the rare book that's up for auction—or else," Brenda said.

"What did the second note say?" Lacy asked.

Brenda opened her mouth to speak, then pressed her lips together and shook her head. Lacy looked to Dwight. "You tell her," Brenda said.

"The second note contained a crime scene

photo from Andy's murder, and said 'this could be you.'"

Lacy gasped, then leaned over and took Brenda's hand. "That's horrible. Who would do such a thing?"

"We're going to find that out," Dwight said.

"What are you going to do until then?" Lacy asked.

"Until this is resolved, I think you should move back in with your parents—or with Travis," Brenda said.

"You can't stay here by yourself," Lacy said.

Dwight was about to agree with her, but Brenda cut him off. "I'm not going to let this creep run me out of my own home," she declared. "I've been manipulated enough in my life—I'm not going to let it happen again."

Was she saying her husband had manipulated her? Dwight wondered. Certainly, Andy Stenson had kept her in the dark about his blackmailing activities and the real source of his income. "We'll put extra patrols on the house," Dwight said. If he had to, he'd park his own car on the curb and stay up all night watching over her.

"Thank you," Brenda said. "In the meantime, I'm going to contact the paper and let them know what's going on. I want whoever is doing this to see that I'm not afraid of him. Besides, if everybody knows what's going on, I'll feel safer. People complain about how nosy everyone is in small towns, but in a situation like this, that could work to my advantage."

"That's a good idea." He turned to look at the letter and envelope still lying on the table. "Let me take care of these, and I'm going to call in some crime scene folks to go over the scene and see if we missed anything. Come with me and we'll call the paper from there."

"All right," she said.

"I'll come with you, too," Lacy said. "Travis should be back from his class soon."

"Give me a minute," Dwight said. He walked

out to his SUV to retrieve an evidence pouch. The women huddled on the porch together, talking softly. Brenda was calm now, but he could imagine how upsetting seeing that photograph had been for her. The person who had left that note wasn't only interested in persuading her to destroy the book. He could have done that with another death threat, or even a physical attack.

No, the person who had left that photo wanted to inflict psychological harm. The man—or woman—had a personal dislike for Brenda, or for women in general, or for something she represented. Or at least, that was Dwight's take, based on the psychology courses he'd taken as an undergraduate. He'd have to question her carefully to determine if there was anything in her background to inspire that kind of hate. With that photograph, the note-writer had gone from a possible annoying-but-harmless prankster to someone who could be a serious danger.

BRENDA RODE WITH Lacy to the sheriff's department, grateful for the distraction that talk about the upcoming wedding provided—anything to block out the horrible image of her dead husband on that note. The photo, more than the threat beneath it, had hit her like a hard punch to the stomach, the sickening pain of it still lingering. Dwight had been shocked, too, though, typical for him, he hadn't shown a lot of emotion. Somehow, his steadiness had helped her step back from the horror and try to think rationally.

Whoever had sent that note wanted to shock her—to terrify her and maybe, to make her reluctant to dig into the reason behind the threat. The letter writer mistook her for a weak woman who would do anything to make the pain go away.

She had been that person once. When Andy dismissed her questions about all the money he was spending on remodeling their home with an admonishment that she didn't need to worry about any of that, she had backed off and accepted his judgment. The idea made her cringe now, but she had been so young, and unwilling to do anything that might mar her happiness.

She wouldn't make that mistake again. Turning away from things that hurt or frightened her only made them more difficult to deal with later. Now she faced her problems head-on, and in doing so had discovered a strength she hadn't known she possessed.

Paige Riddell was waiting in the lobby of the sheriff's department, and confronted Dwight as soon as he walked in. "How dare you treat my brother the way you did this morning," she said before the door had even shut behind Dwight and the two women. "He was trying to help—to do something good—and you shut him down as if he were trying to rob the place. You wouldn't even give him a chance." Her voice shook on the last words—Paige, who to Brenda was the epitome of a tough woman.

Paige, who had taken on Henry Hake's money and position and defeated his plans to build a luxury resort in an environmentally fragile location. Now she seemed on the verge of tears.

"Why don't we go into my office and talk about this?" Dwight gestured down the hallway.

"You didn't have any problem with confronting Parker in public, so we'll do this in public." Paige glanced at Lacy and Brenda. "I'm sure Dwight has already informed you that my brother has been arrested before. He's not trying to hide that. He made a mistake and he paid for it. He went through rehab and he's clean now, and trying to start over—if people like the deputy here will let him."

Dwight frowned, hands on his hips. "If Parker has a problem with something I said, he should come to me and we'll talk about it," he said.

"Parker doesn't want to talk to you. He didn't want to talk to me, but I saw how down he was when he came back from the history museum this morning, so I pried the story out of him. He said you looked at him like you suspected him of planning to blow up the building or something."

Dwight's face reddened. Brenda sympathized with him—but she also related to Paige's desire to protect her brother. Dwight clearly hadn't liked the young man, and his dislike had shown in the encounter this morning. "Paige, does Parker know you're here?" she asked.

Paige turned to her. "No. And when he finds out, he'll be furious. But he's been furious with me before. He'll get over it."

"Why was Parker at the history museum this morning?" Dwight asked.

"Because he's interested in history. It's one of the things he's studying in college. I told him the museum was looking for volunteers and he should apply."

"That's kind of unusual, isn't it?" Dwight

said. "A guy his age being so interested in the past."

"Tell that to all the history majors at his school," Paige said. "Parker is a very bright young man. He has a lot of interests, and history is one of them."

"Any particular type of history?" Dwight asked. "Is he, for instance, interested in the history of World War II? Or local history?"

Brenda held her breath, realizing where Dwight was headed with this line of questioning.

Paige shook her head. "I don't know that it's any particular kind of history. American history, certainly. Colorado and local history, probably. Why do you ask?"

"Does your brother have any history of violence? Of making threats?"

"What? No! What are you talking about?"

"I can check his record," Dwight said.

"Check it. You won't find anything." She turned to Brenda and Lacy. "Parker was convicted for possession of methamphetamine and for stealing to support his drug habit. He was never violent, and he's been clean for three months now. He's going to stay clean. He moved here to get away from all his old influences. He's enrolled in college and he has a part-time job at Peggy's Pizza."

Brenda wet her lips, her mouth dry. "Do you have any yellow stationery at your place?" she asked. "With dancing cartoon flowers across the bottom?"

Paige's brow knit. She looked at Dwight again. "What is going on? If you're accusing Parker of something, tell me."

"Brenda received a threatening note at the museum this morning," Dwight said. "It was written on distinctive stationery." Brenda noticed that he didn't mention the note at her home.

"The only stationery I use is made of recycled paper," Paige said. "It's plain and cream-colored. And Parker didn't write that note. He wouldn't threaten anyone—much less Brenda. He doesn't even know her."

"I'm not accusing him of anything," Dwight said.

"Right." Paige didn't roll her eyes, but she looked as if she wanted to. "I bet you're asking everyone in town about their stationery." She turned to Brenda again. "I know Parker would hate me if he knew I was asking this, but please give him a chance at the museum. He needs constructive things to fill his spare time, and he's a hard worker. And while he's not the biggest guy on the block, he knows how to take care of himself. He would be good protection in case the real person who's making these threats comes around."

Paige's concern for her brother touched Brenda. And she had always had a soft spot for people who needed a second chance. "Tell him to come around tomorrow and fill out a volunteer application. Most of my volunteers are older women—it will be nice to have a young man with a strong back."

"Thank you. You won't regret it, I promise." She squeezed Brenda's hand, then, with a last scornful look at Dwight, left.

Dwight crossed his arms over his chest. "I don't think it's a good idea for you to take on a new volunteer," he said. "Not until we know who's threatening you."

"I know you don't, but I trust Paige's judgment," Brenda said. "She's not a pushover."

"People often have blind spots for the people they love," he said.

She couldn't help but flinch at his words. She had certainly had a blind spot when it came to Andy. Her dismay must have showed, because Dwight hurried to apologize. "Brenda, I didn't mean…"

"I know what you meant," she said. "And I'll be careful, I promise."

The door opened again and Travis strolled in. The sheriff looked as polished and pressed—

and handsome—as ever. If he was surprised to see them all standing in the reception area, he didn't show it on his face. "Hey, Brenda," he said. "What happened to the banner advertising the auction that was hung over Main Street at the entrance to town?"

"What do you mean?" she asked. "It was fine the last time I checked—just yesterday."

"It's not fine now," he said. "It's gone."

Chapter Four

"What do you mean, the banner is gone?" Lacy was the first to speak. "Did someone steal it?"

"I don't know," Travis said. "It was there when I left for my training this morning and it isn't there now."

"Maybe the wind blew it away," Lacy said.

"We haven't had any high winds," Brenda said. "And I watched the city crew hang that banner—it was tied down tight to the utility poles on either side of the street. It would take a hurricane to blow it away."

"Do you think this has anything to do with those nasty letters you received?" Lacy asked.

"What letters?" Travis was all business now.

"Let's take this into your office," Dwight said. "I'll fill you in."

They all filed down the hall to Travis's office. He hung his Stetson on the hat rack by the door and settled behind his desk. Lacy and Brenda took the two visitors' chairs in front of the desk, while Dwight leaned against the wall beside the door. "Tell me," Travis said.

So Brenda—with Dwight providing details—told the sheriff about the two threatening letters she had received: the cheerful yellow stationery, the black marker, the photocopy of the horrible crime scene photo and all about the book the letter writer wanted her to destroy. Travis listened, then leaned back, his chair creaking, as he considered the situation. "What's your take on this, Dwight?" he asked.

Dwight straightened. "I think this guy has a real mean streak, but he isn't too smart."

Brenda turned in her chair to look at him. "Why do you think he isn't smart?" she asked.

"Because if he really wanted to get rid of the book, why not try to steal it? Get rid of it himself?"

"Maybe he knew I'd keep something so valuable locked up," Brenda said.

"Maybe. I still would have expected him to try to get to it before resorting to these threats. There's a lot of risk in writing a note like that—the risk of being seen delivering the notes or of someone recognizing that stationery."

"He—or she—I'm not going to rule out a woman," Travis said, "must think there's a good chance he won't be noticed. Maybe he thinks people wouldn't be surprised to see him around the museum or your house, or he's good at making himself inconspicuous."

"So someone who looks harmless," Lacy said. "That could be almost anyone."

"Where is this book now?" Travis asked.

"It's in my purse." Brenda opened her handbag and took out the small cloth-bound volume and handed it across the desk. "After we found that second letter, we never made it inside to put it in my safe."

Travis opened the book and flipped through it. "I think you're right that this guy isn't very smart," he said. "By demanding you destroy this book, he's focused all our attention on it."

"Or maybe he's really smart and he's trying to divert our attention from what's really important," Dwight said.

Travis closed the book. "I think it would be a good idea to keep this here at the sheriff's department until the auction," he said.

"Fine," Brenda said. "I'll sleep better knowing it isn't in my house."

"You can't go back to your house," Dwight said.

He was giving an order, not making a request, and that didn't sit well with her. "I won't let some nut run me out of my home," she said.

"Someone who would threaten you with that crime scene photo might be serious about hurting you," Travis said. "We can run extra patrols, but we can't protect you twenty-four hours a day. We don't have the manpower. You need to go somewhere that will make it harder for this guy to get to you."

"And where is that?" she asked. "A hotel isn't going to be any safer than my home."

"We can try to find a safe house," Travis said.

"Sheriff, I have a job that I need to do. I can't just leave town and hide out—if I do, then this jerk wins. I won't let that happen."

The two men exchanged a look that Brenda read as *Why do women have to be so difficult?* She turned to face Dwight. "If someone were threatening you like this, would you run away?" she demanded.

He shook his head. "No." He rubbed the back of his neck. "But what about a compromise—somewhere near town where you would be safer, but still be able to work at the museum?"

"Do you know of a place?" Lacy asked.

"I do."

"Not with you," Brenda said. "No offense, but if you want to really start wild rumors, just let people find out I've moved in with you."

Something flashed in his eyes—was he amused? But he quickly masked the expression. "I don't want to start any rumors," he said. "And I'm not talking about moving in with me. But my parents have plenty of room at the ranch, and I know they'd love to have you stay with them. There are fences and a locked gate, plus plenty of people around day and night. It would be a lot more difficult for anyone to get to you there." He let a hint of a smile tug at the corners of his mouth. "And my cabin isn't that far from the main house, so I can keep an eye on you, too."

Brenda recalled Bud and Sharon Prentice as a genial couple who had cheered on their son at every basketball game and helped out with fund-raisers and other school functions. They were the kind of people who worked hard in the background and didn't demand the spotlight.

Lacy leaned over and squeezed Brenda's arm. "You don't really want to go back to your house alone, do you?" she asked.

"Where are you going to be?" Brenda asked.

Lacy flushed. "I think I'll be staying with Travis until this is settled. I'm no hero."

Brenda didn't want to be a hero, either—especially a foolhardy one. "All right," she said. "I'll take you up on your offer. But only for a few days."

"Let's hope that's all it takes to find this guy," Dwight said.

DWIGHT RODE WITH Brenda to his family's ranch west of town. He wasn't going to risk her wrath by coming right out and saying he didn't want her alone on the road, so he made an excuse about having to get his personal pickup truck and bring it into town for an oil change. He wasn't sure if she bought the explanation, but she didn't object when he left his SUV parked in front of her house and slid into the passenger seat of her Subaru. She had packed up her laptop and a small suitcase of clothes—enough for a few days at the ranch. "Do you remember visiting the ranch when we were in high school?" he asked as she headed out of town and into the more open country at the foot of the mountains.

"I remember," she said. "Your parents threw a party for the senior class. I remember being in awe of the place—it seemed so big compared to my parents' little house in town."

"As ranches go, it's not that big," Dwight said. "To me, it's just home." The ranch had been the place for him and his brothers and sister to ride horses, swim in the pond, fish in the creek and work hard alongside their parents. For a kid who liked the outdoors and didn't enjoy sitting still for long, it was the perfect place to grow up. He had acres of territory to roam, and there was always something to do or see.

Brenda turned onto the gravel road that wound past his parents' property, the fields full of freshly mown hay drying in the sun. Other pastures were dotted with fat round bales, wrapped in plastic to protect them from the elements and looking like giant marshmallows scattered across the landscape. She turned in at the open gate, a wrought iron arch overhead identifying this as the Boot Heel Ranch.

"The house looks the same as I remember it," Brenda said. "I love that porch." The porch stretched all across the front of the two-story log home, honeysuckle vines twining up the posts, pots of red geraniums flanking the steps. Dwight's parents, Sharon and Bud, were waiting at the top of the steps to greet them. Smiling, his mother held out both hands to Brenda. "Dwight didn't give any details, just said you needed to stay with us a few days while he investigates someone who's been harassing you," Sharon said. "I'm sorry you're having to go through that, dear."

"Thank you for taking me in," Brenda said.

"I'm sure your mother would have done the same for Dwight, if the shoe had been on the other foot," Sharon said. "I remember her as the kind of woman who would go out of her way to help everyone."

Dwight remembered now that Brenda's mother had died of cancer while Brenda was in college. Her father had moved away—to Florida or Arizona or someplace like that.

"Thank you," Brenda said again. "Your place is so beautiful."

"I give Sharon all the credit for the house." Bud stepped forward and offered a hand. "I see to the cows and horses—though she has her say with them, too. Frankly, we'd probably all be lost without her."

Sharon beamed at this praise, though Dwight knew she had heard it before—not that it wasn't true. His mother was the epitome of the iron fist in the velvet glove—gently guiding them all, but not afraid to give them a kick in the rear if they needed it.

"Let me show you to your room," Sharon said.

"I can do that, Mom," Dwight said. He had retrieved Brenda's laptop bag and suitcase from the car and now led the way into the house and up the stairs to the guest suite on the north side of the house. The door to the room was open, and he saw that someone—probably his mother—had put fresh flowers in a cut-glass vase on the bureau opposite the bed. The bright pink and yellow and white blossoms reflected in the mirror over the bureau, and echoed the colors in the quilt on the cherry sleigh bed that had belonged to Dwight's great-grandmother.

"This is beautiful." Brenda did a full turn in the middle of the room, taking it all in.

"You should be comfortable up here." He

set both her bags on the rug by the bed. "And you'll have plenty of privacy. My parents added a master suite downstairs after us kids moved out."

"Where do you live?" she asked.

"My cabin is on another part of the property. You can see it from the window over here." He motioned, and she went to the window. He moved in behind her and pointed to the modest cedar cabin he had taken as his bachelor quarters. "Years ago, we had a ranch foreman who lived there, but he moved to a bigger place on another part of the ranch, so I claimed it."

"Nice."

The subtle floral fragrance of her perfume tickled his nostrils. It was all he could do not to lean down and inhale the scent of her—a gesture that would no doubt make her think he was a freak.

"I hope you didn't take what I said wrong—about not wanting to move in with you," she said. "It's just—"

He touched her arm. "I know." She had been the center of so much town gossip over the years, first with her husband's murder, then with the revelations that he had been blackmailing prominent citizens, that she shied away from that sort of attention.

"I had the biggest crush on you when I was a kid," he said. "That party here at the ranch— I wanted to ask you to dance so badly, but I could never work up the nerve."

She searched his face. "Why were you afraid to ask?"

"You were so beautiful, and popular—you were a cheerleader—the prom queen."

"You were popular, too."

"I had friends, but not like you. Everyone liked you."

She turned to look out the window once more. "All that seems so long ago," she said.

He moved away. "I'll let you get settled. We usually eat dinner around six."

He was almost to the door when she called his name. "Dwight?"

"Yes?"

"You should have asked me to dance. I would have said yes."

SEEING THE ADULT Dwight with his parents at dinner that evening gave Brenda a new perspective on the solemn, thoughtful sheriff's deputy she thought she knew. With Bud and Sharon, Dwight was affectionate and teasing, laughing at the story Bud told about a ten-year-old Dwight getting cornered in a pasture by an ornery cow, offering a thoughtful opinion when Sharon asked if they should call in a new vet to look at a horse who was lame, and discussing plans to repair irrigation dikes before spring. Clearly, he still played an important role on the ranch despite his law enforcement duties.

Watching the interaction, Brenda missed her own parents—especially her mother. Her mother's cancer had been diagnosed the summer before Brenda's senior year of college. Her parents had insisted she continue her education, so Brenda saw the toll the disease took only on brief visits home.

She had met Andrew Stenson during that awful time, and he had been her strongest supporter and biggest help, a shoulder for her to cry on and someone for her to lean on in the aftermath of her mother's death. No matter his flaws, she knew Andy had loved her, though she could see now that he had assumed the role of caretaker in their relationship. By the time they married, she had grown used to depending on him and letting him make the decisions.

But she wasn't that grieving girl anymore. And she didn't want a man to take care of her. She wanted someone to stand beside her—a partner, not just a protector.

After dinner, she insisted on helping Sharon with the dishes. "That's my job, you know,"

Dwight said as he stacked plates while Brenda collected silverware.

"The two of you can see to cleanup," Sharon said. "I think I'll sit out on the porch with your father. It's such a nice evening."

"You don't have to work for your room and board," Dwight said as he led the way into the kitchen. "I could get this myself."

"I want to help," she said. "Besides, we need to talk. I never got around to notifying the paper this afternoon."

"You can do it in the morning," he said. "The deadline for the weekly issue is the day after tomorrow." He squirted dish soap into the sink and began filling it with hot water.

Brenda slid the silverware into the soapy water. "I've been racking my brain and I can't come up with anyone who would want to harm me or the museum."

"Maybe one of Andy's blackmail victims has decided to take his anger out on you," Dwight said as he began to wash dishes. "We don't know who besides Jan he might have extorted money from, though the records we were able to obtain from his old bank accounts seemed to indicate multiple regular payments from several people."

"Why focus on the book?" She picked up a towel and began to dry. "Part of me still thinks this is just a sick prank—that we're getting all worked up for nothing."

"I hope that's all it is." He rinsed a plate, then handed it to her. "I want to dig into Parker Riddell's background a little more and see if I can trace his movements yesterday."

"Why would he care about me or a rare book?" Brenda asked. "He's a kid who made some mistakes, but I can't see how or why he'd be involved in this."

"I have to check him out," Dwight said.

"I know. I just wish there were more I could do. I hate waiting around like this." She hated being helpless.

"I know." He handed her another plate. They

did the dishes in companionable silence for the next few minutes. The domestic chore, and the easy rhythm they established, soothed her frayed nerves.

Dwight's phone rang. He dried his hands and looked at the screen. "I'd better take this," he said. He moved into the other room. She continued to dry, catching snippets of the conversation.

"When did this happen?"

"Who called it in?"

"What's the extent of the damage?"

"I see. Yes. I'll tell her."

She set the plate she had been drying on the counter and turned to face him as he walked back into the room. His face confirmed her fears. "What's happened?" she asked.

"There was a fire at your house. A neighbor called it in, but apparently there's a lot of damage."

She gripped the counter, trying to absorb

the impact of his words. "How did it start?" she asked.

"They think it's probably arson." He put a hand on her shoulder. "We aren't dealing with a prankster here. Someone is out to hurt you, and I'm not going to let that happen."

Chapter Five

The smell of wet ashes stuck in the back of Dwight's throat, thick and acrid, as he stood with Travis and Assistant Fire Chief Tom Reynolds in front of what was left of Brenda Stenson's house the morning after the fire. The garage and apartment where Lacy lived were unscathed, but the main house only had two walls left upright, the siding streaked with black and the interior collapsed into a pile of blackened rubble. If Dwight let himself think about what might have happened if Brenda had been inside when the fire was lit, he broke out in a cold sweat.

So he pushed the thoughts away and focused on the job. "We found evidence of an accelerant—gasoline—at the back corner of the house," Tom said. "Probably splashed it all over the siding, maybe piled some papers or dry leaves around it and added a match—boom—these old houses tend to catch quickly."

"Do you think the arsonist chose that corner because it was out of view of the street and neighboring houses, or because he wanted to make sure the rooms in that part of the house were destroyed?" Dwight asked.

Tom shrugged. "Maybe both. The location was definitely out of view—someone in the garage apartment might have seen it, but he might have known Lacy wasn't in last night."

"Maybe they knew Brenda wasn't here last night, either," Travis said. He scanned the street in front of the house. "If they were watching the place."

"We'll canvass the neighbors," Dwight said. "See if they have any friends or relatives who have recently moved in, or if they've noticed anyone hanging around or anything unusual."

"What's located in this corner of the house?" Travis asked.

"I think it's where Andy's home office used to be," Dwight said. "I remember picking up some paperwork from him not too long after I started with the department." Brenda hadn't been home, which had disappointed Dwight at the time, though he had told himself it was just as well.

"That's probably where the safe was where Brenda wanted to stash that book," Travis said.

"Probably," Dwight said. "But safes are usually fireproof."

"Maybe whoever did this didn't know about the safe," Travis said.

"Or destroying the book wasn't even the point," Dwight said. "Frightening Brenda into getting rid of the book on her own would be enough for him."

"I guess I'd be frightened right now if I were her," Tom said.

"Brenda's not like that," Dwight said. "I'm not saying she's not afraid—but she's not going to destroy the book, either. This guy's threats are only making her dig her heels in more."

Travis checked his watch. "Thanks for meeting with us, Tom," he said. "I have to get back to the office."

"Yeah, I'd better get going, too," Tom said. "I'll get a copy of the report to you and to Brenda for her insurance company."

Dwight followed Travis to the curb, where both their SUVs were parked. "I'm supposed to meet with the DEA guy the Feds sent to deal with that underground lab we found out at Henry Hake's place," Travis said. "He's had an investigative team at the site and has a report for me."

"Mind if I sit in?" Dwight asked. "I've got a couple of questions for him."

"Sure. I asked Gage to be there, too."

Travis's brother, Deputy Gage Walker, met them at the sheriff's department. Two years younger and two inches taller than his brother, Gage's easygoing, aww-shucks manner concealed a sharp intellect and commitment to his job. "Adelaide told me you two were out at the Stenson place," Gage said as the three filed into the station's meeting room. "I drove by there on my way in this morning. The fire really did a number on the place."

"Tom says they're sure it was arson," Travis said.

"How's Brenda taking it?" Gage asked.

"She's stoic," Dwight said.

"She's been through a lot the past few years," Gage said.

Brenda had been through too much, Dwight thought. And most of it pretty much by herself. She had friends in town, but no one she could really lean on. He got the sense that Andy's betrayal had made her reluctant to depend on anyone. He wanted to tell her she didn't have to be so strong around him—but he didn't want her to take the sentiment wrong.

The bell on the front door sounded, and all conversation stopped as they listened to Adelaide greet a male visitor. Their voices grew louder as they approached the meeting room. "This is Special Agent Rob Allerton." Adelaide didn't exactly bat her eyes at the dark-haired agent, who bore a passing resemblance to Jake Gyllenhaal, but she came close. Gage grinned, no doubt intending to give the office manager a hard time about it later.

Allerton himself seemed oblivious to her adoration—or maybe he was used to it. He shook hands with the sheriff and each of the deputies as they introduced themselves. "Is this your first visit to our part of the state?" Travis asked as they settled in chairs around the conference table.

"My first, but not my last." Allerton settled his big frame into the metal chair. "You people are living in paradise. It's gorgeous out here."

"Don't spread the word," Gage said. "We don't want to be overrun."

"What can you tell us about your investigation of the underground lab?" Travis asked.

"Not much, I'm afraid," Allerton said. "So far our analysts haven't found any illegal drug residue, or really any signs that the lab has been used recently."

"What about World War II?" Dwight asked. "Could it have been used then?"

Allerton frowned. "Want to tell me how you came up with that time period?"

"The local history museum is having an auction to raise money," Travis said.

"Right, I saw the banner the first day I arrived in town," Allerton said.

The banner that had mysteriously disappeared—Dwight had almost forgotten about it in the flurry of activity since then. "One of the items up for auction—probably the most valuable item—is a book detailing a World War II project to produce chemical and biological weapons," Travis said. "Supposedly, the work was done in underground labs in this part of the country."

"No kidding?" Allerton shook his head. "Well, the equipment we found wasn't old enough for that. In fact, some of it appears to have been stolen from your local high school, judging by the high school name stenciled on the glass. There are some indications—marks on the floor and walls—that other equipment or furnishings might have been in that space previously. There's no way of knowing when they were moved. It would be an interesting historical artifact if that were true, but I can't see anything illegal in it."

"Somebody is upset about the book getting out there," Dwight said. "They made threats against the museum director, and last night someone burned down her house."

"That's bad, but I don't see any connection to this lab."

"Seen anybody up there at the site while you

were there?" Travis asked. "Any signs of recent activity?"

Allerton shook his head. "Nothing. I see why this guy, Hake, wanted to build a development up there—it's beautiful. But the ghost town he ended up with is a little creepy."

"Where do we go from here?" Travis asked.

"Me, I go back home to Denver," Allerton said. "If you have questions or need more help, give me a call. I'd love an excuse to get back out here."

He stood, and the four of them walked to the front again. Adelaide smiled up at them. Had she freshened her lipstick? Dwight forced himself not to react. "That didn't take long," she said.

"Short and sweet," Allerton said. "Though I know how to take my time when the job calls for it."

Adelaide blushed pink, and Dwight bit the inside of his cheek to keep from laughing. Allerton said goodbye and let himself out. When he was gone, Adelaide sat back in her chair, both hands over her heart. "Oh my! Did you see those eyes? He looked just like that movie star—what's his name? You know the one."

"Jake Gyllenhaal," Dwight said.

"That's him!" Adelaide crowed.

Travis and Gage stared at him. "You knew that?" Gage asked.

Dwight shrugged. "I like movies."

"He didn't find any signs of illegal activity in that underground lab on Henry Hake's property," Travis said. "That's all I care about."

"Mind if I go up there and take another look around?" Dwight asked. "I might take Brenda with me—she's a historian, or at least, that's her degree. I want to know if she sees anything that might link to the World War II labs that book talks about."

"Fine by me," Travis said. "Technically, it's still a crime scene, since that's where Gage and Maya and Casey were held after they were kidnapped, though I'm going to have to release it back to the owners soon."

"Who are the owners?" Gage asked. "Isn't Henry Hake's name still on the deed?"

"Apparently, the week before he went missing, he signed the whole thing over to a concern called CNG Development. I found out last week when I tried one of the numbers I had for Hake Development. I got a recording telling me the company had been absorbed by CNG, but when I tried to track down the number for them, I couldn't find anything. Then I checked with the courts and sure enough, the change was registered the day before Hake disappeared."

"Coincidence?" Gage asked.

"Maybe," Travis said. "But I'd sure like to talk to someone with CNG about it. The number listed on the court documents is answered by another recording, and the address is a mailbox service in Ogden, Utah."

"Be careful when you head up there," Gage said. "Allerton was right—that place is downright creepy."

TAMMY PATTERSON, the reporter for the *Eagle Mountain Examiner*, agreed to meet Brenda at the museum the morning after the fire. Dwight had tried to persuade Brenda to stay at the ranch and not go in to work that day, but she had refused. Dwight had gone with her the night before to see the house, when the firefighters were still putting out the blaze, but she had wanted to see it herself this morning, alone. She had driven in early and made herself stop at the house and stare at the ruins. Her first thought was that this couldn't really be her place—not the miner's cottage that she and Andy had worked so hard to remodel, the dream home she had lovingly decorated and planned to live in forever.

She had allowed herself to cry for five minutes or so, then dried her eyes, repaired her makeup and driven to the museum. She couldn't do anything about the fire right now, and crying certainly wouldn't bring her house back. Better to go to work and focus on something she could control.

"You don't know how glad I am you called," Tammy said when she burst into the museum, blond hair flying and a little out of breath. This was how Brenda always thought of her—a young woman who was always rushing. "Barry had me reading press releases, looking for story angles. Nobody else ever reads them, so we had this huge pile of them—most of them are about as exciting as last night's town council meeting minutes—which, by the way, I have to turn into a news story, too. So truly, you have saved me."

I'm hoping you can save me, Brenda thought, but she didn't say it—it sounded entirely too dramatic, and might have the wrong effect on Tammy's already-excitable personality. "Glad I could help," Brenda said.

Tammy plopped onto the wrought iron barstool in front of the museum's glass counter and pulled out a small notebook and a handheld recorder. "So what's this story you have for me?" she asked. "You said it was related to the auction, but not exactly? Something juicy, you said. Boy, could I use juicy. I mean, it's great that we live in such a peaceful town and all, but sometimes I worry our readers are going to die of boredom."

Brenda could recall plenty of non-boring news that had run in the paper—surrounding her husband's murder, the wrongful conviction of Lacy Milligan and her subsequent release from prison, revelations about Andy's blackmailing, Henry Hake's disappearance, etc., etc. But she supposed for a reporter like Tammy, that was all old news.

"So, did you find something scandalous in a donation someone made for the auction?" Tammy asked. "Or has some big donor come forward to shower money on you?"

"I wish!" Brenda pulled her own stool closer to the counter. "This has to do with that book we have up for auction—the rare one about the top-secret government plot to make biological and chemical weapons during World War II?"

"I remember." Tammy flipped back a few pages in her notebook. "*The Secret History of Rayford County, Colorado.* Do you have a bidding war? Or you found out the whole thing's a brilliant fake? Or has the government come after you to silence you and keep from letting the secret out of the bag?"

At Brenda's stunned look, Tammy flushed. "Sorry. I read a lot of dystopian fiction. Sometimes I get carried away."

"You're not too far off," Brenda said. "Apparently, someone is trying to silence me."

Tammy's mouth formed a large O. "Your house! I heard about that and I meant to say first thing how sorry I am. But I just thought it was old wiring or something."

"No, the fire department is sure the fire was deliberately set."

Tammy switched on the recorder, then started scribbling in her notebook. "How is that connected to the book?" she asked.

"I don't know. But before the fire, I received two different threatening notes—one here and one at my home, telling me if I didn't destroy that book, I could end up dead."

"Whoa! Do the cops know about this?"

"I told the sheriff, yes." Brenda leaned toward Tammy. "I called you because I want you to make clear in your story that I'm not going to let some coward who writes anonymous notes and sets fire to my house bully me into destroying a valuable historical artifact. If he's so keen to destroy the book, then he can bid on it like everyone else."

"Ooh, good quote." Tammy made note of it. "Where is the book now? Or I guess you probably don't want to say."

"I don't have it," Brenda said. "It's in the safe

at the sheriff's office, where no one can access it until the day of the auction." That wasn't exactly true, but she didn't picture Travis or his deputies taking the book out to show around to just anyone.

"You're right—this is definitely more exciting than the town council meeting," Tammy said. She paused and looked up from her notebook. "I hope that didn't sound wrong. I really am sorry about your house, and those threatening letters would have totally freaked me out."

"They were upsetting," Brenda admitted. "But now that I'm over the first shock, they just make me angry."

"Another good quote." Tammy made a note.

The doorbells clamored and both women turned toward the young man who entered. Parker Riddell froze in the doorway. "Um, you said I should come by about the volunteer work."

"Of course." Brenda pulled a clipboard with

the volunteer application out from under the counter. "Tammy, do you know Parker? He's Paige Riddell's brother. Parker, this is Tammy Patterson. She's a reporter for the local paper."

"Uh, hi." Parker hesitated, then stuck out his hand.

"Nice to meet you." Tammy shook hands, then turned back to Brenda. "I think I have enough here. I'll call you if I think of anything else."

"Thanks, Tammy."

When she was gone, Parker stood staring at the floor for a long moment, not saying anything. "I need you to fill out this application," Brenda said, offering the clipboard.

"Yeah, sure." He took the clipboard and looked around, then slid onto the stool Tammy had vacated. Brenda began straightening the shelves behind the counter, surreptitiously checking out the young man who labored over the forms.

Parker Riddell had the tall, too-thin look of

a boy still growing into a man's body. His skin was so fair blue veins stood out on the back of his hands, while blue-lined tattoos of a skull, a scorpion and a crow—among those she could see—adorned his arms. He hunched over the clipboard, clutching the pen and bearing down on it as he wrote. He looked up and caught Brenda staring, his eyes such a dark brown the iris almost merged with the pupils. "Is something wrong?" he asked.

"You're the first person under the age of forty who's ever wanted to volunteer here," she said. "Well, except for Lacy, but she's my best friend. I'm curious as to why you did it. I'd think it would be boring for you."

He laid down the pen, still holding her gaze. "This whole town is boring for me," he said. "But I like history. I like old stuff." He shrugged. "It's weird, I know."

"It's not weird," Brenda said. "I always liked history, too." She moved to stand across from him. "Are you studying history in school?"

"Just one class this year—at the community college. But I'd like to take more." He signed the bottom of the form and turned the clipboard back to her. "You already know about my record, but it wasn't for a violent crime or anything. And you don't have to let me handle money or anything. I can file stuff or build stuff or, you know, whatever you need."

"Thanks." She smiled. Nothing about this young man seemed threatening. Of course, she had been fooled by people before, but she believed in second chances. "Why don't we start by having you help me pack up everything in our special exhibit room upstairs? I want to install a new exhibit on the war years in Eagle Mountain."

They worked the rest of the afternoon dismantling the installation on historic drugstores—including a mock-up of an old-time soda fountain. It took some time to take down and pack away, and Brenda was grateful for a young, strong and mostly silent helper.

"That was great," she said when she had taped and sealed the last box to go into storage in the basement. "When would you like to come again?"

"I have a class tomorrow, but maybe Thursday?"

"That would be great. Whatever you can manage."

He nodded. "Okay, I have to go to work now." He pulled out his car keys. "I deliver pizza for Peggy's."

"I'll remember that next time I need to place an order."

"Do you need me to carry these boxes down for you before I go?" He indicated the half dozen cartons piled around the exhibit space.

"No, that's okay. I need to decide where I'll put them first. They can stay in here until tomorrow or the next day." She followed him out of the room and pulled a velvet-covered rope across the doorway, then hung a sign that said New Display Coming Soon.

Downstairs, the bells on the door jangled. Brenda checked her watch. Ten minutes until five. She'd have to point out to whoever was down there that the museum would close soon and they would need to return tomorrow. But she took a step back when she recognized the man waiting in the reception area.

"Hello, Brenda." Eddie Carstairs smiled, showing the gap between his two front teeth. His straight black hair angled across his forehead and curled around his ears so that even when he had just had a haircut, he looked in need of another one. He wore a long-sleeved khaki shirt and pants—much like the sheriff's department uniform, sans any insignia. A utility belt equipped with flashlight, nightstick and holstered pistol added to his attempt to appear official. Or at least, that's how Brenda interpreted the look. Eddie had made no secret of his desire to be back in law enforcement since his discharge from the sheriff's department.

"What can I do for you, Eddie?" she asked.

Parker looked from Eddie to Brenda. "Do you want me to hang around a little bit?" he asked.

"No, she doesn't need you to hang around, punk," Eddie said before Brenda could answer. He rolled his shoulders back. "I'm here to protect her from people like you."

"It's all right, Parker, you can go," Brenda said. "And thank you again."

"Sure. See ya." He pushed out the door.

As it shut behind him, Brenda turned on Eddie. "What are you doing here?" she asked. "The museum is closed."

"Your boss, the mayor, decided after that fire at your house, he didn't want to take any chances on the museum, so he hired me as a security guard."

"No one told me anything about this."

He shrugged. "It was just decided. You can call the mayor and ask him, if you like." He leaned one hip against the counter, as if prepared to wait all day.

"I certainly will." She grabbed the phone and retreated into the workroom, shutting the door behind her. She punched in the number for the mayor's office and waited impatiently as it rang and rang.

"Town of Eagle Mountain," a pleasant female voice answered.

"Gail, this is Brenda Stenson. I need to speak with Larry." Mayor Larry Rowe had been elected after Jan Selkirk had declined to run for reelection, running a well-funded campaign with promises of new jobs and opportunities for the town. He wasn't the friendliest person Brenda had ever met, but until now he had left her alone to do her job.

"I think he's still in, Brenda, let me check."

A few moments later Larry answered. "Brenda! What can I do for you?"

"Eddie Carstairs is over here at the museum

saying you hired him as a security guard. Is that right?"

"Well, yes, but he wasn't supposed to start until tonight—after I had a chance to talk with you."

"I'm glad you thought it was a good idea to consult me on this."

Larry's voice hardened. "The city has a valuable investment in that museum, and since you seem to have attracted some unsavory attention, we find ourselves in the position of having to protect that investment."

"So this is all my fault?"

"The arson at your home seems to indicate the threats are targeted at you."

"There's no reason to think the museum is in any danger."

"There's no reason to think it isn't. Eddie came to us and offered his services, and we thought it prudent to take him up on the offer."

She hung up the phone and returned to the front room. "All good?" Eddie asked.

"Fine." She gathered up her purse. "You can follow me outside while I lock up."

"You can leave it unlocked and I'll hang out in here overnight," he said.

"You can follow me outside while I lock up and you can 'hang out' in your car overnight."

She could tell he wanted to argue, but thought better of it. He followed her onto the front porch and watched, frowning, as she locked the dead bolt. "You should be grateful to me for protecting your livelihood," he said.

"I may not have control over much in my life right now," she said, "but at least I get to decide for myself what and who I'm grateful for. Right now, you're not on my list."

The astonished expression on his face was almost worth the aggravation with the mayor. She stalked to her car, started it and had turned down the street toward her home when she remembered she didn't have a home to go to.

Part of her was tempted to keep driving— where, she had no idea. But she had never been one to run away from problems. So she turned around and headed out of town, to the ranch. Time to find out from Dwight how much longer she was going to be stuck in this limbo.

Chapter Six

Parker Riddell cruised slowly down Eagle Mountain's Main Street, careful to stay under the ridiculous twenty-five-mile-per-hour speed limit. He wasn't going to give the local cops any reason to hassle him—not to mention if Paige got a call from the sheriff's office about him, she would go ballistic. He didn't need another lecture about how she was doing him a favor and risking her own reputation and all she had worked for to look after him—yadda, yadda, yadda.

Nobody else was around after nine o'clock at night—talk about rolling up the sidewalks.

This place was like a ghost town. The only cars were parked around Moe's Pub—it and Peggy's Pizza were the only businesses still open. There wasn't a movie theater or even a lousy bowling alley for a hundred miles. Paige always talked as if the lack of anything to do would help him stay out of trouble. Going to the movies and playing video games at the arcade weren't what had gotten him into trouble and she knew it.

But yeah, he was grateful for her—sort of—getting him away from his old hangouts. He'd worked hard in rehab and he didn't want to go back. But man, it wouldn't hurt to have a *little* excitement every once in a while, would it? He turned the corner and drove past the history museum. The pizza in the carrier on the passenger seat beside him was headed to one of Parker's regulars—a guy who worked second shift at the RV factory up in Junction. He ordered a couple times a week. Parker glanced over at the museum as he passed and was surprised to see two cars parked next to the old building. He slowed and craned his neck for a closer look. In the moonlight, he could make out that guy Eddie's pale face behind the wheel of a beat-up Jeep Wagoneer.

Eddie was talking to another man who had positioned his black SUV cop-style, so the drivers were door-to-door. What were they doing at the museum this time of night?

He made his delivery. His customer, Jason, tipped him a five, which was really decent of him. Parker slipped the five in his wallet and the rest of the money in the pouch for Peggy, then headed back toward the museum. He parked up the block and made his way in the darkness, sneaking up behind the two vehicles. He wasn't doing anything wrong, he reminded himself. Brenda clearly hadn't liked this Eddie fellow, and Parker owed it to her to make sure the guy wasn't ripping her off.

Parker hadn't thought much of the cop wannabe, either. It hadn't taken too many brains to figure out that Eddie was the guy Paige had talked about as the reserve deputy who had been fired and was trying to make trouble. And he'd looked at Parker like he was a dog he wanted to kick.

Parker heard Eddie and the other guy a long time before he got close enough to see them in the dark. Obviously, they weren't worried about being overheard. But Parker couldn't make out everything they said, just phrases that drifted on the night breeze.

"I'm taking care of it," Eddie said.

A mumble from the other guy.

"You don't have to worry. I know how to handle this. That's why you hired me, right?"

The other guy said something and they both laughed. Parker needed to get closer, to hear the whole conversation. He moved carefully, keeping to the shadows from a row of bushes alongside the alley where the cars were parked.

He didn't see the pile of debris set out for

trash pickup until it was too late. He stumbled right into it, sending boxes and cans tumbling down, making a racket that could probably be heard a block away.

"Hey!" Eddie shouted.

The other man started up his SUV and sped away. Parker lurched to his feet and tried to run, but Eddie was on him, shoving him back onto the ground, the barrel of his pistol pressed to the side of Parker's face. "What are you doing sneaking around here?" Eddie demanded.

"I saw the cars. I wanted to make sure everything was all right."

Eddie shoved Parker's face further into the gravel. "Were you trying to steal something? I'll bet that's what you were doing. You 'volunteered' so you could check the place out and come back later and help yourself."

"No!" Parker squirmed, trying to free himself.

"Shut up." Eddie shoved the gun harder into

Parker's cheek. "Maybe I ought to shoot you now and do everyone here a favor."

"DO YOU THINK you could get away from the museum one day and go with me up to the Eagle Mountain Resort site?" Dwight asked as he and Brenda did dishes that evening. Dinner had been grilled steaks on the back patio, and Brenda had done her best to smile and join in the conversation, but he could tell she was distracted. No surprise—she was probably worried about her house, and about whoever had targeted her.

"Why do you want me to go up there with you?" she asked.

"When we rescued Gage and Maya and her little niece, Casey, from those kidnappers last month, they were being held in an underground chamber on the resort land," he said.

"Yes, I heard about that." She added a dried plate to the stack on the kitchen table.

"What you probably didn't hear is that next

to the chamber where they were held was another underground space that looked as if it had been used as a laboratory. The DEA has been investigating it, and hasn't found any sign of illegal activity. Now I'm wondering if it could be related to the labs the government established in the area to work on biological and chemical weapons—like that book talked about."

She stuck out her lower lip, considering. "The book does talk about some of the laboratories being underground—in old mines or caves. What does the DEA say?"

"They don't think any of the equipment is old enough, but they're not historians. I thought if you had a look, you might interpret things differently."

"But Wade and Brock kidnapped Maya and Gage and Casey," Brenda said. "And they're dead—right?" Finding out that the two men who ran the town's successful outdoor store were behind the kidnappings, and responsible for the murders of Maya's sister and brother-in-law, had shocked the town.

"They're dead, but we suspect they were working for someone else."

"The same person who's been threatening me?"

"Maybe," he said. "But maybe not."

She fell silent, mechanically drying plates and glasses and silverware, but Dwight couldn't shake the feeling that something was wrong. When the last dish had been put away, he turned to her. "Something's bothering you," he said. "Is it the threats or your house, or something else on top of all that?"

"I think that's enough to bother anyone," she said.

"It is. But if it would help to talk about it—if you need someone to listen to you, I'd like to be that person."

She straightened the dish towel she had just hung on the handle of the oven. "It will prob-

ably sound silly, especially considering everything else that has happened."

"I've never thought of you as particularly
silly," he said. "What's happened?"

"The mayor—without consulting me—
decided to hire Eddie Carstairs as a security
guard for the museum. At a time when our
budget is so squeezed we don't know if we'll
be able to keep the doors open, he decided to
spend money on this. And when I objected,
he insinuated this was all my fault—that I had
somehow put the museum property in danger."

Anguish colored the flood of words. He
waited until she fell silent once more and said,
"I can see why you're upset. The mayor isn't always the most diplomatic person." Larry Rowe
had spent a lot of money and effort on his
campaign for the office, but once elected, he
had developed a reputation as a no-nonsense
administrator who did whatever it took to get
what he wanted.

"To make things worse, Eddie showed up

while Parker Riddell was still at the museum and treated him horribly. It was embarrassing."

"So Parker volunteered today?" Dwight kept his voice neutral, though he didn't like the idea of Brenda working closely with the troubled young man. Parker might be sincere in his desire to make a fresh start, but did Brenda have to be part of that?

"Yes, and he was wonderful. He's a very serious, quiet young man, and he's sincerely interested in history." Her shoulders sagged. "And I think he's lonely. There aren't a lot of people his age in this town for him to hang out with."

"It's great that you want to give him a chance," Dwight said. "Just...be careful."

"I will, I—"

His phone rang, interrupting her. "Sorry," he muttered, and took the call.

"Eddie Carstairs just hauled in Parker Riddell," Gage said when Dwight answered.

"Eddie says he caught him trying to break into the history museum."

Dwight glanced at Brenda. "I heard that," she said.

"I'll be right down," Dwight said, and ended the call. He started toward the door, Brenda close behind him.

"I'm coming with you," she said.

"Brenda—"

"I'm in charge of the museum. And I agreed to take Parker on as a volunteer. If he was breaking in, then I need to address this, too."

He saw no point in trying to argue with her. "All right," he said. "Let's go see what this is all about."

BRENDA HAD NEVER been in this part of the sheriff's department—in the level below ground, and the single holding cell outside the booking area. Dwight had escorted her through a maze of locked doors without comment, until they stood outside the small cell where Parker sat, staring out from behind the bars. The young man looked angry, but behind the anger, she detected fear. Fear he was doing his best to hide, but she could see it.

"Brenda, I swear I didn't do the things he says," Parker said.

"Shut up, punk." Eddie, who had been talking with Gage at the far end of the booking area, turned to face them, frowning when he saw Brenda. "What are you doing here?" he demanded.

"I'm in charge of the museum," Brenda said.

"I'm going to check on a few things," Gage said to Dwight. "I'll leave you to look after things here."

Dwight nodded, then addressed Eddie. "What happened?"

"I caught him sneaking around in the alley, trying to pry open one of the windows," Eddie said.

"That's a lie!" Parker said.

"Quiet," Dwight ordered. "You'll have your turn in a minute."

"I did my job," Eddie said. "I cuffed him and brought him in."

"Why didn't you call nine-one-one?" Dwight asked.

"I didn't need backup to handle one punk."

Brenda balled her hands into fists. If Eddie used that word—*punk*—one more time, she might have to slap him.

"You aren't authorized to arrest anyone, much less bring them in and demand they be put in a cell," Dwight said.

Eddie folded his arms in front of his chest. "I made a citizen's arrest," he said. "And apprehending a potential thief falls under my duties as security guard at the museum."

"He's lying," Parker said again, his voice less strident, more pleading.

"I'd like to hear Parker's side of the story," Brenda said.

Dwight turned to Parker. "All right, let's have it."

"I was driving home from delivering a pizza down the street from the museum. I saw this guy—" He pointed to Eddie. "He was sitting in a Jeep that was parked alongside the museum, in that alley. He was talking to another guy, in a black SUV."

Eddie leaned toward them, clearly about to object. Dwight held up a hand to stop him. "Let him continue."

"This afternoon, when I left the museum, I could tell Brenda was uncomfortable with this guy—Eddie—being there," Parker said. "I thought I should make sure he wasn't causing trouble."

Eddie laughed. "Oh, you'd know trouble, wouldn't you?"

Parker glared at him, then continued. "I wanted to hear what he and the guy in the SUV were talking about. I tried to get close enough to hear, but I tripped over some garbage and he heard me. The guy in the SUV took off and Eddie tackled me and held a gun to my head and demanded to know what I was doing there. He threatened to shoot me."

"Drama queen," Eddie said. "He's making that up. Wants you to feel sorry for him."

"Who was in the SUV?" Dwight asked Eddie.

"The mayor stopped by to see how things were going," Eddie said. "He knew Brenda was upset with me being there. We heard somebody rattling around in the alley and I ran back and caught Parker here trying to pry open a window. I figure he was going to steal some stuff to sell."

"No! I didn't try to break in," Parker said. "Go look for yourself. You won't find my fingerprints anywhere."

"You were probably wearing gloves," Eddie said.

"Then where are they now?" Parker asked.

Eddie shrugged. "You probably threw them away."

"Then they'd be in the alley, wouldn't they?"

"Eddie, did you threaten Parker with a gun?" Dwight asked.

"Of course not. I know better than that."

Brenda didn't believe him. Eddie wouldn't look Dwight in the eye—instead, his gaze kept darting to Parker.

"Look at my face." Parker pressed his cheek up against the bars. "You can see the bruises and cuts from where he pushed my face into the gravel." He turned to display the other cheek. "And there's a mark on this side where he held the gun barrel."

Brenda and Dwight leaned forward to view the faint round cut. "That could be from a pistol," Dwight said.

"The punk threatened me," Eddie protested. "I had a right to use force."

"You need to leave now, Eddie," Dwight said. "I'm going to take you upstairs and I'll deal with you later." He glanced at Brenda. "Will you be all right for a few minutes?"

"Of course."

Eddie opened his mouth, then closed it again. He followed Dwight to the first locked door, but before Dwight could unlock it, it opened, and another deputy escorted Paige Riddell inside.

"What is going on?" Paige demanded. Then she saw Parker in the cell and rushed over to him.

"Rich, take Eddie upstairs and see him out," Dwight said.

"I didn't do anything," Parker said. "I was trying to help."

"I believe you," Brenda said.

"I'm going to send someone over to the museum to check," Dwight said. "If we don't find anything, we'll let you go."

"Eddie Carstairs is a liar and a weasel," Paige said. "He always has been. And he's never liked me, ever since I turned him down when he asked me out."

"I swear, I thought he and that guy in the SUV were up to something," Parker said. "That's the only reason I stopped."

"Next time you see something suspicious, call us," Dwight said. "Don't investigate on your own."

Parker looked at the floor, saying nothing. Brenda imagined for someone in his position, only recently out of jail and rehab, calling the cops wasn't the first line of action that came to mind.

The door opened again and Gage stepped in. "I checked the museum," he said. "I can't find any sign of tampering with any of the windows."

"Any gloves lying around anywhere?" Dwight asked.

"No. But I did find where it looks like Eddie and Parker scuffled—and two sets of tire tracks."

"Did you get a good look at the man in the other car?" Dwight asked Parker. "Was it the mayor?"

"I couldn't see him very well," Parker said. "And I've never met the mayor, so I wouldn't know what he looks like."

"Clearly, Parker is telling the truth," Paige said. "You need to let him go."

"Brenda, do you want to press charges for trespassing?" Dwight asked.

"No." She shook her head.

"I think you should be charging Eddie with assault," Paige said.

"No, Paige," Parker said. "I just want to get out of here."

Dwight unlocked the cell, and Parker stepped out. He stopped in front of Brenda. "Thanks for believing me," he said.

"I do believe you." She lifted her chin. "I'm a good judge of character—not always, but most of the time. I think Eddie was the one lying, not you."

The four of them left together. "I'll take you home," Dwight said to Brenda.

She waited until they were in his SUV before she spoke again. "Why was Eddie lying?" she asked.

"I can't say for sure," Dwight said.

"But you have a theory. Tell me."

He sighed. "Eddie has always wanted to be the hero. I think, his first night on the job, he wanted to catch a burglar, prove it was a good idea for the town to hire him. But he always goes overboard. That's why Travis fired him."

"I think you're right," she said. "And I'm glad Travis fired him. He thinks wearing a gun makes him better than everyone else, and that's a dangerous attitude."

"Are you going to let Parker volunteer at the museum again?" Dwight asked.

"Yes. He did a great job for me today." She angled toward him, and studied the side of his face, illuminated by the dashboard lights. "Sometimes you have to go with your gut and trust people. And don't remind me I trusted Andy when he didn't deserve it."

"I wasn't going to say anything."

"I was younger then," she said. "And I was still grieving for my mother when we married. And later—later, I think I knew something wasn't right. It was why I kept questioning him about how we could afford all the work we had done on the house. But I was in love, and I wanted to believe him."

"I understand," Dwight said. "And I'm glad everything you've been through hasn't made you cynical."

"Not about everything," she said. "Though I don't trust as easily."

"That's all right. One thing being a cop teaches you is persistence."

She studied him, surprised by the word choice. "What is that supposed to mean?" she asked.

"It means I'm going to earn your trust. One

of these days you're going to let down your guard with me and let yourself feel again."

She looked away. She didn't want to ask him what he thought she would feel. She could see it there, shining in his eyes. Dwight Prentice didn't think of her as just another crime victim who needed help. When he looked at her, he saw something more. He was letting her know that, but she wasn't sure what she was supposed to do about it. She wasn't ready to let down her guard with him or any other man. She wasn't ready to fall in love. The message Dwight had just sent her let her know he wasn't going to settle for less.

Chapter Seven

The next morning, Dwight met with Travis to review the previous night's events. "I spoke with the mayor," Dwight said. "Eddie's story about him stopping by last night checks out, though he says he doesn't know anything about Parker Riddell being there."

"What about the rest of Eddie's claim?" Travis asked. "Was Parker trying to break into the museum?"

"I don't think so," Dwight said. "I think the kid really was trying to sneak up on him and the mayor and Eddie overreacted—as usual."

"Gage didn't find any sign of an attempted break-in at the museum," Travis said.

"Brenda said she thought Eddie was lying, and I tend to agree with her," Dwight said. "He wouldn't look me in the eye."

"They could have chosen a better person for the job, but I don't think the town was wrong to hire a watchman for the museum," Travis said. "If the person who threatened Brenda thinks the book might be there, it's the next logical target."

"Brenda gave an interview to Tammy Patterson yesterday," Dwight said. "She said she told Tammy to make sure she stated in the article that the book was locked up at the sheriff's office."

"Good idea," Travis said. He leaned back in his chair, frowning. "Forensics didn't turn up anything on the notes. We did find the banner—ripped to pieces with a knife, probably a pocketknife—and stuffed into the Dumpster behind Moe's Pub. Nothing to go on there. The arson report on Brenda's house didn't turn up anything new, either."

"So we're back to wondering who wants that book destroyed and why," Dwight said.

"How's Brenda holding up?" Travis asked.

"Amazing. She's determined not to let this guy get to her. I thought later this morning I'd take her up to Eagle Mountain Resort and show her the lab—see if she spots any historical details the DEA missed."

"That's not going to prove a connection between what happened up there with Gage and Maya and what's going on with Brenda now," Travis said.

"No, but it might point us somewhere—to some collector and someone involved in the original project."

"When are you going?"

"She had some work to do at the museum this morning, then we're going to head up there," Dwight said. "Meanwhile, I want to take a look at that book."

"It's in the safe downstairs," Travis said.

"Make sure you sign it back in when you're done."

"Yes, sir."

Dwight retrieved the combination to the safe, then got the book and sat down at his desk with it. After the first few pages, he struggled to keep going. The writer—S. Smith—had managed to take a potentially exciting subject and make it dry as sawdust. So he was relieved when the phone on his desk rang.

"There's a man here who wants to speak to you," Adelaide said. "A Professor Gibson."

Dwight closed the book and set it aside. "Send him in."

The professor was about eighty years old, thin and slightly stooped, with a full head of white hair and faded brown eyes peering from behind horn-rimmed spectacles. "The young woman at the newspaper suggested I talk to you," he said, peering into the office.

"Which young woman is that?" Dwight asked.

"Tammy? The reporter?" He stepped into the room and looked around.

"Why don't you sit down, Mr. Gibson." Dwight stood and closed the door behind the man.

"Val. Val Gibson." He lowered himself carefully into the chair across from Dwight's desk. "I'm a retired professor of history at Colorado State University."

Dwight returned to his seat. "Why did Tammy suggest you contact me?"

"She called me to get some information for a story she's working on—something to do with the government's activities in the state during World War II—Project Razor. She was researching the topic online and found an article I had written and realized I was a local. I retired to the area seven years ago."

"Project Razor?" This piqued Dwight's interest. "Do you mean the project to develop chemical weapons for use in the war?"

"Not just chemical weapons—biological ones, too."

"I'm not sure I'm clear on the difference," Dwight said.

"A chemical weapon uses a chemical agent to inflict harm," Gibson explained. "So, for example, mustard gas in World War I or sarin gas. A biological weapon uses a pathogen, such as smallpox or anthrax."

"Aren't those against the Geneva Convention or something?" Dwight asked.

"The Geneva Convention of 1925 did ban the use of biological and chemical weapons," Gibson said. "But by World War II almost every major power, including the United States and Great Britain, had development programs in place. We don't believe the biological agents were ever used, but it wasn't until 1972 that a UN treaty was formed that forbade production of biological weapons—and even then, not every country is a signatory."

"How effective are biological weapons?"

Dwight asked. "I mean, they sound terrible, but can't people be vaccinated or something?"

"Are you vaccinated against Q fever and tularemia?" Gibson asked.

"I've never even heard of them."

"Many of the agents used in biological warfare are obscure. As weapons, they can be devastating, but their effect isn't immediate, delivery methods are awkward, and you can't account for individuals who might have a natural immunity. So they're not seen as very practical for large-scale warfare. Still, there is some concern that terrorists could use them as another way to wreak havoc—release a vial of botulism spores in the air-conditioning system of a large office building and you could kill a lot of people and create a panic."

Dwight held up the book. "Are you familiar with this?"

"I'm very familiar with it," he said. "I have reason to believe that copy you're holding belongs to me."

Gibson spoke calmly, his expression pleasant. "Why do you think that?" Dwight asked.

"That young man—a lawyer—asked to borrow it years ago. Andrew Stenson. I was reluctant to lend it, but he was very persuasive. By the time I tried to get it back, he was dead." Gibson shrugged. "I tried to contact the widow, but the person who answered the phone said she was too upset to talk to anyone. They promised to look for the book and return it to me. I never heard anything back. I probably should have pressed the issue more, but it seemed petty, under the circumstances."

Was he telling the truth? Dwight couldn't tell. On one hand, maybe he was—Andy must have gotten this obscure title from somewhere. On the other, maybe this was a less-violent ploy to get hold of the book.

"Why did Andy Stenson want this book?" Dwight asked.

"He said he needed it for research he was doing on a case. He didn't elaborate, and I didn't pry. It's been my experience that lawyers as a group are fairly tight-lipped. Which I suppose is as it should be."

"Why didn't you say anything to Brenda Stenson when you saw that the book was up for auction?" Dwight asked.

"I didn't know it was up for auction until Tammy told me about it yesterday afternoon," Gibson said. "I don't take the local paper."

Again, maybe true—maybe not.

"I'll admit I haven't read the book," Dwight said. "It's a little…dry."

Gibson chuckled. "I suspect the author had written one too many government reports. It reads much like one. But as far as I've been able to determine, the information in the book is factual."

"Is there anything in there that might lead someone to want the book destroyed?" Dwight asked. "Something that incriminates an individual or casts a bad light on someone?"

"Destroyed?" Gibson looked puzzled.

"Someone sent Mrs. Stenson threatening notes, ordering her to destroy the book—or else. What kind of stationery do you use, Professor?"

"I have never threatened Mrs. Stenson, Deputy. And I'm not the sort of person who would ever destroy a book, or ask someone else to—especially not a valuable collector's item, like that one." He straightened. "And I don't use stationery. Who does in these days of emails and text messaging? I may look like a dinosaur to you, but I'm not."

Dwight remained skeptical. "You said Tammy contacted you because of an article you wrote about the project?"

"Yes. I've thought of writing a book about the history of biological and chemical warfare. The research has been a hobby of mine for some time now."

"Do you know where in Rayford County Project Razor took place?"

"I haven't been able to discover that, no." He

nodded toward the book on Dwight's desk. "All that says is that abandoned mines were used for the laboratories, but considering how many of those are in the area, that isn't much of a clue."

"Do you know of anyone alive today who was involved in this research?" Dwight asked.

"No. From what I can gather, the scientists involved were in their thirties and forties at the time. That would make even the youngest over a hundred years old."

"Then it's not one of them threatening Mrs. Stenson. Maybe a child or grandchild?"

Gibson shook his head. "There's nothing in the book to implicate anyone. As I recall the author, Mr. Smith—which I suspect is a nom de plume—didn't use any real names in his book. There's a disclaimer in the front that says so."

Dwight nodded. He had skipped over the book's front matter, but he had a vague recollection of an author's note. He'd go back and read it later. "Maybe this book isn't even the point," he said. "It could be a distraction to keep us from looking at the real reason for the threats."

"Why did Mrs. Stenson decide to auction the book?" Gibson asked.

"The museum she directs is in financial trouble. When she found the book in her late husband's belongings, she researched it online and saw how valuable it was, so she decided to sell it and use the money for the museum. She's been collecting donated items from others to auction, as well."

Gibson nodded. "I suppose I would rather see the book used for something like that than for personal gain."

"You could always bid on the book yourself."

He smiled. "My days of having that kind of money to spend on a hobby are gone. I lucked on to the book at a secondhand shop in Denver a good twenty years ago. I think I paid seven dollars for it at the time."

"Are you going to ask Mrs. Stenson to return the book to you?"

"I don't think so. I wasn't savvy enough to ask her husband for a receipt or any other proof of the loan. That was my own foolishness." He stood. "Now that you've told me what Mrs. Stenson intends to do with the book, I'm happy to see it used for those purposes." He gave a wry smile. "As you observed, it's not exactly light reading material—and I never was one for owning things I wouldn't use or enjoy. Though I hope the threats toward Mrs. Stenson don't continue."

"We're watching the situation closely." Dwight walked with the professor toward the front of the station.

He was surprised to find Brenda waiting in the reception area. She stood as he approached. "I'm ready to leave when you are," she said.

"Brenda Stenson, this is Professor Val Gibson," Dwight said. "He—"

"I have some expertise in the history of biological and chemical weapons development in the US," Gibson said. "I wanted to offer my services to law enforcement in regard to the book that I understand has been the subject of threats to you."

"You know something about the threats?" Brenda asked.

"No, only about the book and its subject matter," Gibson said. "I'm afraid I wasn't much help." He nodded to her, then turned to Dwight. "Feel free to contact me if you have any questions."

As soon as the professor had left, Brenda moved closer to Dwight. "What was that about?" she asked.

"I'll tell you on the drive up to the resort. Come on." He led the way out the back of the building to his cruiser.

She waited until they were belted in and he had started the engine before she spoke again. "Why did the professor really come to see you?" she asked.

"You don't believe what he told you?" Dwight asked.

"You were about to say something about him when he interrupted." She sat back in the seat. "Don't ever play poker, Dwight. Your face is full of tells."

"You should have been the attorney in the family," he said. "You'd be good at interrogating witnesses. But before I answer your question, tell me if you've ever heard of Professor Val Gibson before."

"No. Who is he?"

"He's the man who owned that book before Andy. He said Andy wanted to borrow it to do some research for a case he was working on. The professor never saw the book again and had put it out of his mind until Tammy called him up yesterday to interview him for the article about the threats being made against you."

"Whoa, back up a little. Andy stole the book from the professor?" In addition to being a blackmailer, was her late husband a thief, also?

"I don't think he intended to steal it—I think he borrowed it and was murdered before he could return it. Then it just kind of fell through the cracks."

She nodded. "Does he want the book back? Is that why he came to you?"

"That may have been his intention originally, but after he learned about the auction to raise money for the museum, he seemed okay with that. And he admitted he didn't have any proof that it ever belonged to him."

"Maybe learning someone is threatening me because of the book made him think twice about wanting to own it," she said.

"That may have had something to do with it, too," Dwight said.

"I still don't understand how he ended up

talking to you," she said. "Why not contact me directly?"

"Apparently, Tammy called him for some information for the article she's writing about the book and the threats to you," Dwight said. "She found him through an article he wrote about the top-secret government labs in Colorado during World War II and learned he was in the area. He told me he retired here seven years ago. When she learned he knew all about the book, she suggested he get in touch with me."

"But he wasn't able to help you?"

"He seemed to know a lot about what was in the book, and about the government's activities in general, but neither of us could think of any reason someone would want the book destroyed. He told me the author used pseudonyms for all the people who were involved in the project, and it's doubtful any of them are alive anymore, anyway."

"So he really wasn't much help."

"No. He doesn't know where the work was done, although he did say the weapons they developed were never used."

"I suppose that's comforting—sort of," she said.

"Everything okay at work this morning?" he asked.

"Eddie wasn't there and nothing was missing. No new threatening letters. So I'd call it good."

"Have you heard from Parker?"

"No, but I don't expect to. He said he had classes today." She shifted toward him. "I know you aren't crazy about Parker, but I really like him. I think at heart, he's a good kid."

"There's such a thing as being too trusting," he said.

"And there's such a thing as being too cynical," she shot back.

To her surprise, he grinned. "Guilty as charged. It's part of the job."

He looked so comfortable in his uniform,

here in this cruiser, surrounded by the tools of his trade. "When we were growing up, I never would have pegged you as a future cop," she said.

"What did you think I would do?" he asked.

"I don't know—ranching, I guess. Or maybe business." He had always made decent grades, and been the serious, thoughtful type.

"I thought about both of those," he said. "But I have an uncle who is a small-town police officer in Wisconsin, and I always admired that. And I didn't want to sit behind a desk at a job where I'd be bored."

"I can't think law enforcement in Eagle Mountain is that exciting—at least most of the time."

"Some days are more of an adrenaline rush than others—for me, the pace is about right. And my ranching background comes in handy when we have to put cows or horses back in pastures."

She laughed. It was a local joke that the

weekly sheriff's department activity reports printed in the local paper always contained a number of calls to put livestock back in pastures.

"It's good to hear you laugh, in spite of everything that's happened," he said.

"I'm still alive. I still have a job and friends, and I'm going to get through this." Saying the words made her feel stronger—and they were true. The threats were frightening, and she had lost things in the fire she would miss forever, but she still had so much.

"Yes, you are," he said. They fell silent as the cruiser headed out of town. Soon houses gave way to a solid wall of evergreens on either side of the road, and beyond that the red-and-gray cliffs of the mountains. "Have you ever been up here, to Eagle Mountain Resort?" Dwight asked.

"Once—they had some kind of ribbon-cutting or ground-breaking and I attended with Andy. That seems like a lifetime ago." It had been four years—she had definitely been a different person, then.

"What did you think?" he asked.

"That it was a shame to build fancy houses that would stay empty half the year in such a beautiful spot. I kept that opinion to myself. It didn't seem wise to criticize the man who was pretty much paying for the roof over my head and the food on my plate."

"You haven't been up here since?"

"No. Though I've heard it's a ghost town now. Paige and her group think it's an eyesore. Before Henry Hake went missing, they were lobbying him to restore the property to its natural state.

"I guess everything is in limbo until Hake is found."

"Hmm."

It was the kind of non-comment that made Brenda suspect Dwight knew more about Hake's disappearance—or about the future of the resort—than he was willing to say.

That was probably part of being a cop, too—knowing things you couldn't talk about. But she didn't care. She had never been particularly fond of Henry Hake, and though she missed his regular donations to the museum, she couldn't pretend to grieve for him now that he was probably dead. As for his proposed resort, it would either be developed or not, and there were plenty of other people in town—like Paige Riddell and her environmental group—to worry about it. Brenda had other things to focus on—the upcoming auction, securing funding to keep the museum open, and finding a new place to live.

Dwight pulled the cruiser into a paved drive and parked in front of a pair of massive black iron gates. The gates stood partially open, remnants of yellow-and-black crime scene tape flapping from the crossbars. "Those gates aren't supposed to be open," Dwight said. He put the cruiser in Park and got out to examine the gates. A moment later, he was back. "Someone cut the lock," he said.

"Didn't you say the DEA had been up here, investigating?"

"I don't think they would have been so sloppy as to leave a broken lock hanging on the gate." He eased the vehicle through the opening and up the drive. Brenda studied the boarded-up buildings, crumbling foundations and dying landscaping that was all that remained of the proposed luxury development. Dwight steered around a waterfall of rock that spilled down an embankment and she knew without asking that this was where Wade Tomlinson and Brock Ryan had died, after they had left Gage and Maya and little Casey for dead.

Dwight stopped in front of a Quonset hut partially built into the hillside. "The lab is in here," he said.

She followed him out of the vehicle and walked to the entrance. The door—a massive metal rectangle with no window—leaned against the side of the hill. "Travis had that removed," Dwight said. "He didn't want anyone to end up locked inside—accidentally or on purpose."

Brenda repressed a shudder. "I'm glad he did. I'm not sure I'd want to go in if it was on there."

"Come on. I'll show you the lab." Dwight switched on his flashlight and led the way inside. The first room was a large, bare space, the dirt floor packed down and clean, save for a handful of dry leaves that skittered across the space, stirred by their entrance. A second door stood open at the far end of the room, and as they drew closer, Brenda realized it had been removed from its hinges also.

Dwight played the beam of the flashlight into the next room and swore under his breath. "What's wrong?" she asked, and moved up beside him to look inside.

"The place is cleared out," he said. "There

was a workbench and tables and lab equipment in here before."

The space—with a floor of concrete, not dirt, and chains hanging from the ceiling that might have once held light fixtures—had been swept clean, not so much as a speck of dirt on the floors or walls, which were completely bare, except for a fly that crawled up one wall. "Maybe the DEA took everything away," she said.

"They didn't bother to mention it to us." He pulled out his phone and took several pictures.

Brenda's gaze shifted to the opening at the far end of the room. "Is that where Gage and Maya were held?" she asked.

"Yes." Dwight led the way across to it. Brenda hung back. "It's all right," he said. "There's nothing in here. It's pretty much like that first room—empty."

He was right, of course. It wasn't as if she were sightseeing in a torture chamber. Still, she had to make herself cross the room to stand beside him. "Why are these rooms even here?" she asked.

"I don't know," he said. "Storage, maybe." He shone the light through the opening, and they both leaned in to examine the space. The beam of light illuminated a dirt floor, concrete walls—and something suspended from the ceiling—a suit of old clothes or a dummy or—

"Don't look." Dwight shoved Brenda back as the realization of what she was looking at hit her.

"Is that a body?" she asked.

He put his arm around her and hurried her toward the door. "We need to get down and call for help," he said. "I think we might have found Henry Hake."

Chapter Eight

Dwight stood beside his cruiser as the EMTs loaded the body into the back of the ambulance. Brenda sat inside, pale but silent, staring through the windshield toward the emergency vehicle's strobing lights. She hadn't said much of anything since they'd driven away from the resort to call for help, then headed back to wait for the sheriff and others to arrive. Dwight had tried to think of something to say to comfort her, but he hadn't been able to come up with anything. She was shaken but not hysterical, which pretty much described his own feelings.

When the EMTs had closed the doors behind them and driven away, Travis came over. "What made you think it was Henry Hake?" he asked.

"The suit," Dwight said. "Henry always wore those brown suits—I don't know. Something about it just struck me as him. I probably should have verified before I blurted it out like that."

"The coroner will verify, but it's probably Hake," Travis said. "There was a wallet in the back pocket, with Hake's driver's license. A money clip with the initials *HH*, but no money."

"Where's he been all this time?" Dwight asked. "It's been weeks."

"The body looked sort of—mummified," Travis said. "I didn't do a really thorough examination, but there wasn't any obvious sign of trauma. We'll have to wait for the medical examiner's report."

"When we got here, the lock on the gate had been cut and it was open," Dwight said. "And everything's been cleaned out of the lab."

"I saw that. I'll contact Allerton, but I don't think the DEA did that."

"Yeah. I'm guessing whoever left Hake's body cleaned out the lab, too. They must have known we'd find him."

"They've had plenty of time to cover their tracks," Travis said. "They could have left the area—even the country—by now." The ambulance drove past and he signaled the crime scene techs to move in. "There goes my theory that Wade and Brock killed Hake."

"You thought that?" Dwight asked.

"Why not? They killed Maya's sister and brother-in-law and would have killed Gage and Maya if they'd had the chance."

"But why?" Dwight asked. "What was in it for them?"

"I haven't come up with an answer to that yet." He glanced toward Dwight's SUV. "Why the threats to Brenda? Why burn down her house?"

"Do you think what's going on with her

is connected in some way to Hake's disappearance and what happened with Maya and Gage?" Dwight asked.

Travis rubbed the back of his neck. "I don't know, but it feels that way. This is a small county—historically very low crime, and nothing very serious. And now we have a crime wave. Everything else has been related to this property, starting with Andy Stenson's murder three and a half years ago."

"Andy is the one who first got hold of that book the guy who's targeted Brenda wanted destroyed," Dwight said. "He told Professor Gibson he needed it to research a case. I'm wondering if the case had something to do with Hake—and if Andy was killed because he found out something he shouldn't have."

"Ian Barnes never said why he killed Andy," Travis said. "But he told Lacy he needed to kill her because she knew too much—something she didn't even realize the significance of. She has no idea what he was talking about."

"We've always assumed Maya's sister and brother-in-law were killed because they saw Wade and Brock with Henry Hake," Dwight said.

Travis nodded. "But what if they saw something else?" He glanced over his shoulder toward the Quonset hut. "Something to do with that lab, maybe."

"Every time we pull at one thread in this case, everything gets more knotted up," Dwight said.

"But we're going to keep pulling until we find the solution to the puzzle," Travis said. "I'll finish up here. You take care of Brenda."

Dwight returned to the SUV. "What now?" Brenda asked.

"If you feel up to it, you'll need to make a statement. We just need to get down your account of what happened for the case file."

She nodded. "I can do that."

"It's better to do it now, while it's fresh in your mind."

"Fine. I'll do it now."

"After that I can take you home. To my home, I mean."

"All right."

He started the cruiser and headed back toward town. Beside him, Brenda was still as a statue, not making a sound. She was too calm. Finding Henry Hake's body that way must have shaken her—it would have shaken anyone. It had shaken *him*. Yet she showed no emotion at all. Not reacting was probably a defense mechanism, especially considering how much tragedy she had faced recently. But walling off emotions never worked for long, and the fallout could be worse than giving in to tears now.

BRENDA DICTATED HER statement to Dwight, getting through the ordeal by pretending the events of that morning had happened to someone else. Every time she closed her eyes, she could see the shapeless figure in the baggy suit hanging there, twisting slowly in the breeze… Then she would snap open her eyes, take a deep breath, and focus on something else—the crooked diploma on the wall behind Dwight's desk, the chipped paint near the doorway of his office, the dust on the toes of her own shoes.

When she had signed the printed statement, he ushered her back to his car and drove out to his parents' ranch. She appreciated that he didn't try to talk to her. She didn't have anything to say. She felt empty—hollowed out and fragile, less woman than paper doll.

It wasn't until they passed the turnoff to his parents' house that she stirred. "Where are we going?" she asked.

"I'm taking you to my place," he said. "I thought you might appreciate the peace and quiet there. My mom means well, but she tends to hover."

"Thanks." She had to speak around the lump in her throat. His thoughtfulness touched her.

She cleared her throat. "I'm sure you have work to do," she said. "I shouldn't be keeping you from it."

"I don't have anything urgent right now." He glanced at her. "I want to make sure you're all right."

"I'm fine." She spoke the automatic lie she had been using for years now. The assurance kept people from prodding too deeply. She was keeping it together so they didn't have to worry.

Dwight said nothing, merely pulled up to his cabin and parked. The square cedar-sided cabin featured a porch across the front, and a gray tabby cat asleep in a rocking chair beside the door. The cat stood and stretched at their approach. "This is Otis," Dwight said, pausing to scratch behind the cat's ears before he opened the front door.

Otis purred like an engine humming along and followed them into the cabin, long tail twitching. "Oh, this is nice," Brenda said, stopping three steps into the front room. She wasn't sure what she had expected—something utilitarian and maybe a little worn, filled with hand-me-down furniture and the clutter of a bachelor life. Instead, the open, high-ceilinged room had the comfortable Western vibe upscale design magazines strived for, with a layer of authenticity that welcomed a visitor to sit down and kick off her shoes.

A Persian carpet in shades of red, black and blue covered the worn wooden floor, and a cast-iron-and-soapstone woodstove dominated one wall, flanked on either side by big windows that offered a view of golden hayfields and the mountains beyond, the peaks dusted with the autumn's first snow. A caramel-colored sofa and two matching armchairs were arranged around a table made from a slab of wood worn smooth by years of use. A flat-screen TV on an oak sideboard was the chief reminder that this was a modern home and not some backcountry retreat.

"Make yourself at home," Dwight said, motioning toward the sofa. "I'll fix us something to drink."

Not waiting for a reply, he headed toward the kitchen, which was separated from the living area by a massive island. Brenda moved to the sofa and sat, looking around at the shelves of books between the windows and the artwork on the walls—pen-and-ink drawings of elk, moose and other wildlife interspersed with paintings of rodeo cowboys. She leaned closer to peer at one of the paintings, of a young man in jeans and chaps carrying a saddle, a number pinned to the back of his leather vest. "Is that you?" she asked, when Dwight rejoined her in the living room.

"Me a long time ago," he said. "The artist is a family friend." He handed her a short, squat glass filled with ice and a dark liquor, and sat on the sofa beside her—close, but not touching.

She studied the drink. "What is this?"

"A brandy old-fashioned."

"Dwight, it's only one in the afternoon."

"Drink it. You need it after what you experienced this morning. I know I do." He took a long swallow of his own drink.

She took a tentative sip. It was sweet—and had a definite heat as it went down. She set the glass on the edge of the table and continued to look around the room.

"We should talk about what happened," Dwight said.

She turned to him. "I gave you my statement."

He frowned. "I don't mean the events that occurred—I mean, what's going through your head right now."

"Nothing's going through my head right now."

"And you don't think that's a problem?"

"I don't know what you mean."

He scooted forward to the edge of his seat and set his drink beside hers on the table. "Then I'll be frank. I'm worried about you. You've been through more awful things in the past few days—much less the past four years—than most people have to suffer through in a lifetime. Yet you go on as if nothing has happened. That's not normal."

She stiffened. "I'm not the hysterical type," she said. "And I did break down after Andy died." For months she had barely been able to function. She didn't want to go back to those helpless, out-of-control days.

He moved closer. "I'm not saying you have to get hysterical," he said. "But it's okay to let yourself feel. To acknowledge that some awful things have happened. And that it's not fair."

She nodded. She'd heard this advice before—read it in the books she turned to after Andy's death, told it to herself even. But taking the advice and letting go wasn't so easy. "Life isn't fair," she said. "I know that. And I don't see any point in dwelling on it."

Dwight took her hand. "I know you're tough.

I admire that about you. But if you keep trying to bear the weight of all this by yourself, I'm afraid you're going to crumble."

His fingers twined with hers, so warm and strong. She held on in spite of herself, wanting to draw courage from him. "I don't know what you want from me," she whispered.

"I want you to trust me enough to believe that you don't have to put up walls between us," he said. "You've been hurt and it's okay to acknowledge that."

She stared down at her lap, her vision blurring. "I'm afraid," she said.

"Afraid of what?"

"Afraid if I let myself think about how awful things are right now, I'll start crying and never be able to stop."

"I'm no expert," he said. "But I think sometimes, if you let the hurt out, it makes room for good things to fill up that space."

"What good things?" The words came out

harsh and full of bitterness she hadn't wanted to acknowledge. "I don't have a home. I may not have a job soon. Some maniac is threatening to kill me." Her voice broke. "I've never been so afraid or felt so alone."

He drew her to him, his arms a firm barrier to keep away harm. She buried her face against his shoulder, her tears flowing unchecked. She hated breaking down like this, yet it was such a wonderful release to do so. As the first wave of emotion subsided, she became aware of him stroking her back and gently kissing the top of her head. A different sort of emotion welled within her—a fierce awareness of Dwight as a man. New tears flowed, but these were tears of relief that after all she had been through, she could still feel the things a woman should feel—she was still alive and capable of desire and passion.

She tilted her face up to his and found his lips, pressing her body more firmly against his. He responded with an urgency that matched her own, pulling her onto his lap, one hand caressing her hip while the other cradled her cheek. She wrapped both arms around him, her breasts flattened against his chest, her mouth open, tongue eagerly exploring his mouth, reveling in thrilling, too-long-forgotten sensations shooting through her.

She rocked her hips and smiled as he let out a low groan, his erection hard and hot between them. He pressed his lips against her throat and spoke in a voice ragged with lust. "We'd better stop now unless you want it to go further," he said.

"Oh, I want it to go further." She trailed one hand along his cheek, the prickle of five-o'clock shadow along his jaw sending a fresh wave of heat through her. "I want you. I think I have for a while now, I just wasn't ready to admit it."

He grinned in answer and shoved to his feet,

carrying her with him. She laughed, and he gripped her tightly and kissed her until she was dizzy and breathless. "Put me down," she pleaded, laughing.

"Oh, I'm not putting you down," he said. "Not until neither one of us is capable of standing."

He stalked toward the bedroom, her legs wrapped around his waist, his fingers digging into her buttocks. He didn't release her until they both collapsed onto the bed, and then only to begin stripping off her clothes as she tore at his shirt and pants.

Only when they were both naked, cuddling together side by side, did their fury give way to tenderness—still urgent, but more deliberate, each intent on savoring the moments. She trailed her fingers across the taut skin of his shoulders, tracing the contour of muscle and bone, memorizing the shape and sensation of him. He did the same, brushing kisses along her jaw and down the column of her throat, his tongue following the swell of her breasts and dipping into the valley between them, then sliding along to suck at first one breast and then the other, until she was quivering and all but whimpering with need.

She reached between them and grasped him, satin-smooth and hot, all but pulsing in her hand. "Do you have any protection?" she asked.

In answer, he gently pried her fingers from him and slid over to the side of the bed and took a condom from the drawer of the night-stand. He ripped open the package and rolled on the rubber, the movement leaving her dry-mouthed and ready to pounce on him.

Instead, he lay back and pulled her on top of him. "Ready to go for a ride?" he asked.

"Oh, yeah." She lowered herself over him, closing her eyes against the exquisite plea-sure of him filling her. When she opened them again, she found him smiling up at her, his eyes full of such wanting and tenderness that it all but undid her. She began to rock, gently at first, then with more movement, drawing out their pleasure, holding back as the need built between them. He grasped her hips, encouraging her, and they began to move together, thrust and withdrawal, advance and retreat, until she shuddered, her climax overpowered her, filling and overflowing. "Dwight!"

His name still echoed around them as he found his own release. He pulled her close to him and kissed her hard, then rolled with her onto his side, where they lay, still connected, his eyes reflecting all the wonder she felt. "Feel better now?" he asked.

She laughed. "I do." She kissed the end of his nose. "Thank you."

"No thanks needed," he said. "I'm just glad you're here."

"Me, too." She hadn't felt all that glad to be anywhere in a long time, and though he wouldn't let her thank him for it, she was more than grateful that he had given her back this part of herself—this ability to feel so alive and whole.

Chapter Nine

Dwight never got around to taking Brenda up to the main house that night. His parents could see his cruiser parked at his cabin from their house, and he suspected they would draw their own conclusions about Brenda's whereabouts. He was happy to have her stay with him, and he wasn't about to put a damper on the new closeness they shared by suggesting she leave. Whatever barriers she had erected before had melted away somewhere between her flood of tears and the passion they had finally given in to.

She slept in his arms that night and woke

early to make love again, a satisfying, leisurely coupling that left him so ridiculously happy he was afraid the grin he wore was permanently etched on his face.

He made breakfast while she showered, and when she joined him in the kitchen, smelling of his soap, damp tendrils of hair curling around her face, he had to focus to get his breathing under control. "Did you find everything you needed?" he asked, deliberately playing it cool.

"Oh, I think so." She moved to the coffee-maker and filled a cup.

Dwight turned back to the frying pan. "How do you like your eggs?" he asked.

"However you want to cook them. I'm not picky."

He scrambled eggs and made toast, aware of her eyes on him. Conversation, which had before now been easy with her, was apparently choked off by the lust that hovered like a cloud around him. How was it that at thirty, he could be reduced to the incoherence of adolescence?

She smiled when he set the plate down in front of her. "I could get used to this," she said.

"So could I."

She said nothing, but polished off the breakfast as if she were famished—which she probably was, considering they had never gotten around to eating last night. When she finally pushed her plate away, she sighed. "That was delicious."

"Thanks," he said. "I'm no gourmet, but I manage to feed myself."

She put her chin in her hand and studied him, her silent scrutiny making him nervous. "What is it?" he asked. "Why are you looking at me that way?"

"I'm just wondering why it is you're still single."

That definitely wasn't a question he had expected. "Last I heard, being single isn't a crime," he said.

"Of course it isn't. But you're an attractive man with a good personality, a nice home, a good job. There are plenty of unattached women in this county who would love to go out with you. But I can't remember you ever being in a relationship with any of them. Why?"

"You worried I'm gay?"

The pink flush that spread across her cheeks made her look even sexier. "Um, no."

"I've dated," he said. "I'm just discreet about it."

"Then you definitely have a talent for subterfuge. It's not easy keeping a secret like that in this town."

"I like to keep my private life private."

"So do I," she said. "But I haven't had much luck with that, so far. The *Examiner* might be broke by now if it weren't for me and those I'm close to supplying them with juicy headlines."

"You're not responsible for the things Andy did," he said gently.

"No, but I'm part of them. I can't get away from that. And as you might imagine, it hasn't made me eager to trust another man."

"You can trust me."

"Can I?" The expression in her eyes had hardened. "Haven't we already established that you're good at deception?"

"I don't deceive people I care about."

"I'm sorry. I didn't mean to suggest that." She looked away. "It's not you who's messed up, it's me."

"Don't say that." He leaned across the table toward her. "There's nothing wrong with you. You're perfect."

A choked laugh escaped her. "Oh, no I'm not."

"You're perfect for me. I've always thought that." He straightened. "Maybe you're the reason I'm not married. I was waiting for you."

"Dwight." She shoved out of her chair and stood, backing away from him. "Last night—

what happened between us was amazing. But that doesn't mean I'm ready for more, I—"

"I know." He resisted the urge to move toward her, forcing himself to remain still, to rely on his words to reach her. "I'm not asking for anything. But you asked me an honest question—I figured I owed you an honest answer."

She considered this for a moment, then nodded. "All right. But what happens now?"

"Now I think I should take you to work." He stood, the movement slow and easy, as if she were an easily frightened animal. "Your car is still there, right?"

"Right. I'll get my things." She started to turn away, then stopped. "Thank you for being so understanding."

Oh yeah. He was understanding all right. Understanding that when it came to Brenda Stenson, he was pretty much at her mercy. Not a position he liked to be in.

BRENDA PRIDED HERSELF on keeping her emotions in check, but Dwight's declaration that he had been waiting for her had left her reeling. While last night had been an incredibly pleasurable and yes, healing, experience, she hadn't been prepared for what amounted to a declaration of love from a man she had always considered as taciturn and frankly, hard to read.

And now she had to sit here beside him in his cruiser and pretend that her emotions weren't all over the place. Wouldn't it be nice if she could have even a single day that wasn't full of drama? She'd almost forgotten what that was like.

Her morning didn't get any better when Dwight drove her to the museum and she spotted Eddie Carstairs seated on the bench beside the front door. "What is he doing here?" she asked as Dwight pulled his cruiser to the curb.

"Let's find out," Dwight said.

Her first instinct was to tell him that she

could take care of Eddie herself, but maybe it wasn't a bad idea to have a witness to back her up if things got heated. For whatever reason, Eddie seemed to have the mayor on his side, and since the town council was Brenda's employer, she ought to tread carefully.

"Hello, Eddie," she said as she climbed the steps to the front porch of the museum. "Did you need something?"

"Just keeping an eye on things," he said.

"I thought you were a night watchman," she said.

He ignored her, turning instead to Dwight. "I heard there was some excitement yesterday afternoon, up at Eagle Mountain Resort," he said.

"I imagine the news is all over town by now," Dwight said. But he didn't elaborate on what that news might be.

Eddie shifted from foot to foot. "Pretty funny to find Henry Hake up there after all this time, don't you think?" he said.

"I don't know of anyone who found it amusing," Dwight said.

Brenda opened her mouth to tell Eddie to get lost when he turned to her. "You were there, weren't you?" he asked.

"Yes." She crossed her arms over her chest. "But I don't have anything to say to you about it."

"I heard the body was practically mummified," Eddie said. "I figure his killer stashed him up there in one of those caves up on the cliffs. The Indians used to do that and the cool, dry air just desiccates the body. Sort of like beef jerky."

"I wouldn't know about that," Brenda said.

Eddie turned to Dwight again. "You must know how he died," he said.

"If I did, I wouldn't share it with you," Dwight said.

"You ought to think twice about that," Eddie said. "I know a lot of people in this town, see a lot of stuff. I might have information that could help you."

"If you have information, tell me what it is," Dwight said. "But the exchange doesn't work both ways."

The two men glared at each other like two roosters about to face off. Brenda was grateful when a new arrival interrupted.

"Hi, Brenda," Parker Riddell said as he headed up the walkway. "You said you might need help with that new display today."

"Yes, Parker." She offered him her warmest smile. "I'm glad to see you."

The two slightly older men studied the younger one as he mounted the steps to stand by Brenda. "Hello, Deputy, Eddie," Parker said.

Dwight greeted Parker, but Eddie only nodded, his lip curled in a sneer. Neither man gave any indication of budging. "Eddie, Dwight, you need to take this conversation elsewhere," Brenda said. "Parker and I have work to do."

Dwight's eyes met hers. She remained firm, but gave a slight nod, to show she wasn't holding anything against him. "Come on, Eddie," Dwight said. "Let's get out of Brenda's hair."

"This is public property," Eddie said. "I have a right to be here."

"Yeah, but if you waste the whole day standing around here, people are going to get the wrong idea," Dwight said.

"What do you mean?" Eddie asked.

"They're going to figure you don't have anything better to do. That you're too washed up to get a job."

"I have a job," Eddie said. "I'm establishing my own private security company."

"Right. Then go find some more clients. Don't stand around here harassing Brenda."

"I'm not harassing her. I—"

"Eddie!" Brenda snapped the word, more than tired of this conversation. "Get out of here or I'll call the mayor and tell him you're interfering with museum business."

She could tell he wanted to argue with her, but he set his jaw and stalked down the steps and across the yard to his Jeep.

"I'll be going, too," Dwight said, keys in hand.

"I'll see you later." Then, without another look back, she walked into the museum. For now, at least, this was her domain—the kingdom she ruled without a consort. Yes, it was lonely, but there was a kind of security in that loneliness, a way to keep her heart safe even if her head argued she was being stupid.

Parker followed Brenda inside, where she greeted Emma Waide, who had been volunteering at the museum since it first opened. "We're going to be working on the new exhibit if you need anything," she said.

"How is school going?" she asked Parker as they climbed the stairs to the second floor.

"It's okay. My history class is pretty interesting. Just basic American history, but still, the professor is good."

"The classes will get more interesting if you pursue the degree," she said. "You can home in on areas of particular interest."

"I like the World War II era. There was so much happening all over the world back then."

The exhibit in progress was just as she had left it the day before yesterday, with most of the material they would display still in boxes. Brenda consulted the plans she had drawn up. "I hope you're ready to work," she said. "I need you to move some shelves and tables around for me. Some of them are pretty heavy."

"No problem."

For the next two hours, they worked arranging the space. Parker proved both strong and fast, and able to work well without supervision—in other words, a dream volunteer. "I'd never get this done so quickly without your help," she said as she surveyed the newly arranged furnishings. "Now all we have to do is set out the items on display. Later today I'll work on printing out all the labels and signs."

"This is the fun part," Parker said as he opened a carton and lifted out a World War II-era uniform. "Like opening Christmas presents."

"It is sort of like that," Brenda agreed. "I've seen all this stuff before, but it's been packed away for a while. And some of it has never been on display. People give us things all the time that we have to save for the appropriate exhibit." She set a canteen and mess kit side by side on a shelf.

"What do we do with the clothes?" Parker asked, as he laid out a navy uniform next to the army gear.

"We have mannequins we'll need to dress," she said. "We'll save them for last."

After another hour, they had everything unpacked and arranged. Brenda might move some items later, after she had time to consider the flow of the exhibit. The idea was to display things in a logical order that led visitors from one area of the room to the next. They retrieved the mannequins from her workroom and arranged them in the center of the room, the navy man clutching a pair of binoculars, his army counterpart holding a field radio.

"It looks pretty good," Parker said as he and Brenda stood in the doorway, surveying their work.

"It will look even better when the signs and labels are up. And I may add a few things in. Sometimes after a new exhibit goes up, someone will come in and donate something that fits the theme."

"What about that book you're auctioning?" he asked. "The one about the secret labs that were here in the county in World War II?"

She shook her head. "It's far too valuable—and apparently, controversial—to display."

"Do you think I could see it some time?" he asked.

"Why do you want to see it?" she asked.

He shrugged. "To try to figure out what all the fuss is about, I guess."

"The sheriff has the book and it's going to stay with him until the auction."

"Yeah, I guess that probably is best. Have you had any more threatening letters?"

"No. I hope the article in the paper will scare off whoever wrote the letters. I tried to make it clear that I was immune to threats."

"I hope you're right and you scare him off," Parker said. "And don't just make him angry and want to try harder."

His words sent a shiver through her. She watched him out of the corner of her eye as they moved empty boxes back into storage and swept up the room. Maybe he was only curious about the book and concerned about her—but what if he had other motives?

She said goodbye to him and the afternoon volunteer and prepared to lock up the building and leave herself. She hated feeling this way—untrusting and suspicious. Was Dwight's cynicism rubbing off on her? If that was the case, she wouldn't thank him for it.

Chapter Ten

"We have the coroner's report on Henry Hake." Travis distributed copies around the conference table, two days after Dwight and Brenda discovered the body. "There was a fair amount of deterioration, but he's ruled out physical violence as the cause of death. He found no sign of gunshots, knife wounds or asphyxiation."

Dwight skimmed the paperwork, flipping over to the end of the report. Next to "Cause of Death" was a single word: *Inconclusive.*

"Does that mean it's possible Hake wasn't murdered?" Gage asked.

"We can't rule out murder," Travis said. "Especially considering how the body was found. But the coroner did say the body was strung up after death—and that it hadn't been hanging where we found it long."

"We knew that already," Gage said. "The Feds only left the place three days ago."

"Maybe Hake was poisoned," Dwight said. "One of those poisons that leaves the body in a relatively short time."

"Did the coroner say how long Hake had been dead?" Gage asked.

"Approximately seven weeks—maybe a little more," Travis said.

"So he died not too long after he disappeared," Dwight said.

"The coroner did find evidence of heart disease," Travis said. "It's possible Hake was kidnapped and the stress brought on a heart attack. The kidnappers panicked, ditched the car and hid the body."

"Then why not keep the body hidden?" Dwight asked.

"Maybe because now we don't have a way of linking Hake to the killer?" Gage asked. "They think they're in the clear."

"Hake's car was found near the resort, and his body was found on the resort," Travis said. "The Hoods died because they saw something at the resort they shouldn't have. Wade and Brock kidnapped Gage and Maya and Casey and imprisoned them at the resort."

"So the resort is key to solving all of this," Dwight said. "What is going on up there that someone is willing to kill to protect?"

"We need to know that," Travis said. "And we need to know who." He consulted his notes. "Gage, you saw a black SUV at the resort when you were fired on. Casey reported seeing a similar SUV—and two men in dark suits— when she went for help. Wade and Brock were talking to those men before they were killed."

"So the suits were running the show." Gage nodded. "Two strangers in suits are going to stand out around here, where pretty much everybody wears casual clothing unless they're going to a wedding or a funeral. Even the bankers and lawyers seldom put on a jacket and tie."

"So why haven't we been able to find them?" Dwight asked. "And why haven't we been able to find whoever is threatening Brenda?" Their canvass of the neighborhood had turned up not a single clue to help them find the arsonist who had burned down her house.

"The only link we can find between Brenda and the resort is the fact that her late husband was the lawyer who represented the development company," Travis said.

"And he was killed because of something he saw or said or did that didn't please his murderer's boss," Gage said.

"Ian Barnes was Henry Hake's bodyguard," Travis said. "But in talking with him before he died, I got the impression that there was someone above Hake who was calling the shots.

My feeling is that that mysterious someone ordered Andy Stenson's murder."

"Why did Hake need a bodyguard?" Gage asked.

"Because he was afraid of the people over him?" Dwight asked. "He thought they were dangerous?"

"Or because those people had enemies who were dangerous," Travis said.

"Henry Hake had enemies of his own," Gage said. "Paige Riddell's environmental group didn't make any secret of their loathing for him and his development. And let's not forget his own lawyer, Andy Stenson, who was probably blackmailing him."

"So maybe Hake did order the hit on Andy," Dwight said. "But then who kidnapped Hake?"

"If he was kidnapped," Travis said, "we don't have any proof of that."

"When a guy disappears and his car ends up in a ravine—but his dead body is found hanging in an underground chamber a month later—that didn't all happen of his own free will," Gage said.

"And the coroner said no physical trauma," Dwight said. "So it's not as if Hake somehow managed to escape his car, only to die of his injuries later."

"And what—someone found the body and decided to hang it up as some kind of sick joke?" Gage asked.

Dwight shrugged. "Stranger things have happened."

"Right now all we have are a lot of questions and no answers," Travis said. "But maybe I'll get some answers this afternoon. I have a meeting with the new owners of the Eagle Mountain Resort property."

Dwight and Gage exchanged looks. "What was that company's name again?" Dwight asked.

"An investment group called CNG Development," Travis said. "I'm meeting with their representative on the property at two."

"Who is CNG Development?" Dwight asked.

"That's what I'm hoping to find out," Travis said. "As far as I can determine, at least some of the principals were silent partners in the original development. Before Hake disappeared, they signed an agreement with him to take over control of the property."

"How come nobody else knew about this?" Gage asked. "I mean, the way gossip spreads in this town, I would have thought someone would have said something."

"I think they kept it deliberately low-key," Travis said.

"Do they plan to go ahead with developing the property?" Dwight asked.

"That's one of the questions I'm going to ask them." Travis consulted his notes again. "What else do we have going on right now?"

"I'm working the high school basketball tournament this evening," Gage said. "Maya says the girls' team has a good chance of winning."

Gage's fiancée, Maya Renfro, had snagged a position teaching English at the high school when another teacher's husband was transferred. A former avowed city girl, she had thrown herself into small-town life and signed on as assistant coach of the girls' basketball team.

"Dwight, what are you working on?" Travis asked.

"I'm going to take another look at that book of Brenda's, see if I can figure out what Andy might have been looking for when he borrowed it from the professor. And I'm going to touch base with Brenda and see who has made a bid on the book so far."

"I thought the auction wasn't until next Saturday," Travis said.

"It isn't, but she said bidders had the option of mailing in a bid ahead of time. I want to know if anything has come in that might raise a red flag."

"There's a reception next Friday night where

people can view all of the items up for auction, including the book," Travis said. "I want as many of us as possible there, keeping our eyes open for anyone suspicious."

Everyone was beginning to look suspicious to Dwight—not a feeling he especially liked.

"We still have our regular patrols," Travis said. He read off their assignments for the day and they dispersed.

Dwight resisted the urge to drive by the museum first thing. Brenda had been polite but decidedly cool toward him since he'd made the mistake of revealing his true feelings to her yesterday morning. So much for the honesty women said they wanted.

But maybe that wasn't a fair judgment, either, he admitted. Brenda had made it clear she wasn't ready for a relationship, and he could see how his comment might make her think he was trying to rush things.

Instead of saying he had remained single because he was waiting for her, he should have shared another bit of truth: staying single was a lot easier than navigating the land mines inherent in any relationship.

WITH THE AUCTION fast approaching, Brenda spent the next few days working long hours at the museum, proofing the final copy of the auction catalog and updating listings on the website she had established as new items continued to come in. The work needed to be done, but when she was being honest with herself, she admitted that staying late at the office gave her an excuse to avoid Dwight. She couldn't think clearly when she was with him, what with her body demanding to be back in his bed and her mind focused on the benefits of sticking close to a man with a gun and a desire to protect her. She could shut up her mind with a reminder that she had received no more threatening letters. Her body, awakened from long dormancy, wasn't so easily reasoned with. Better to avoid the object of her lust until she had gained a little perspective.

Work was one thing that allowed her to focus. The interest and support from the people of Eagle Mountain and the surrounding county touched her. Surveying the growing collection of items in her workroom, it seemed as if half the residents of the area had raided basements and attics for great-granddaddy's miner's lamp or great-grandmother's Victrola to contribute to the museum's fund-raising efforts.

But their generosity wasn't going to be enough. The money the auction would bring would keep things going for a few more months, at most, but an ongoing donor was needed to insure continued operation—and Brenda's continued employment. In addition to getting ready for the auction, she continued to send letters to potential sponsors, both corporate and private.

She was composing such a letter, long after

the museum had closed, on the Tuesday be-fore the auction when a pounding on the door broke her concentration. A glance out the win-dow showed a distinguished-looking man in a dark suit standing on the porch. Annoyed but curious, she opened the door. "The mu-seum is closed," she said. "You're welcome to come back tomorrow morning after nine." She tried to see past him, into the parking lot. Wasn't Eddie supposed to be around some-where, doing his security guard duties? She hadn't seen any sign of him all evening.

"I'm here to see Mrs. Brenda Stenson." He offered a smile that transformed his expres-sion from businesslike to breathtaking. Of av-erage height and build and in his forties, he had the thick dark hair and piercing gray eyes of a matinee idol. "Would that be you?"

"Yes." She maintained her composure under the force of his movie-star smile. "What can I do for you, Mr...?"

"Brownley. Robert Brownley. Could we go

inside to talk? It's awkward, standing here on the doorstep."

If she admitted she was alone in the building, would that make her more vulnerable? She had certainly been alone in the museum with strangers many times, given that she operated with a skeleton staff. But always before, that was during regular business hours, when another person could have walked in any time. She should tell Mr. Brownley to come back tomorrow.

"I have a financial proposal to make," he said. "I would have come earlier, but my business demands my attention during working hours. I saw your car out front and decided to take a chance that you were here."

He certainly looked like a man who had money to give away—his deftly tailored suit, gleaming leather shoes and even his haircut advertised wealth—and the black SUV parked beside her Subaru was a brand she was sure retailed for close to $100,000. That didn't mean he wasn't a serial killer, but could she really afford to pass up the chance that he was going to offer up a much-needed donation to the museum? She stepped back, holding the door open wider. "Come in."

He strode past her, the spicy fragrance of his cologne trailing in his wake. He admired the photographs on the walls and the books displayed on the shelves. Brenda perched on the high stool next to the cash register, keeping the glass display case that served as the front counter between them. "What can I do for you, Mr. Brownley?" she asked.

"I'm interested in one of the items you have listed for auction," he said.

"Oh." She tried not to show her disappointment. "You're welcome to make an early bid online, or attend the live auction Saturday night," she said.

"I'm prepared to make a preemptive bid now," he said. "I'll beat any subsequent bid you might obtain."

"What's the item you want to bid on?"

"It's a book. *The Secret History of Rayford County, Colorado.* An esoteric item, I admit, but I'm a collector, and you know how collectors are obsessive about completing our collections."

The hair on the back of her neck stood at attention at the mention of the book, but she remained cool. "We've had quite a bit of interest in that item," she said. "As I'm sure you're aware, it's quite rare."

"Yes." Did she imagine that his smile held less warmth? He looked around the room, scanning the titles on the shelves, as if he expected to find the book there. "And as I explained, I am prepared to meet or beat any other bid you receive, provided the volume meets with my expectations. I'd like to see it and assess its condition."

"The book is in a secure location. Off-site," she added. "All the auction items will be on display at the reception Friday evening, which you're welcome to attend. And of course, you can see everything the morning of the auction."

No smile now. Without it, his expression was forbidding. "I'm prepared to offer a substantial sum to acquire this volume," he said. "I don't think it's too much to ask for a private showing ahead of time."

"That isn't possible," she said. "The book isn't here. It isn't anywhere I can get to it."

"That's a very poor way to do business," he said.

"That may be your opinion, but it's how we've chosen to handle it." She pulled her cell phone from her pocket. "I think you'd better go."

He scowled at the phone, then turned and stalked out. When the door had slammed behind him, she laid the phone aside and slumped on the stool. She hated confrontation. But even worse, she hated people who tried to push her around.

Five minutes later, the jangle of the doorbells had her grabbing up the phone again, heart pounding. Dwight stepped into the room, and the sight of his lanky figure in the familiar khaki uniform left her weak with relief. "Everything okay here?" he asked.

She laid down the phone and smoothed her damp palms on her skirt. "Fine. I'm just working late on auction stuff."

"Who was that in the black Land Rover that just went tearing out of here?" he asked.

"A man who wanted to place an auction bid. I explained he could go to the website or attend the live auction Saturday."

Dwight's alert posture didn't relax, and his gaze remained fixed on her. "What did he want to bid on?"

She opened her mouth to tell him, but what came out was, "Oh, it doesn't matter." She began shutting down her laptop. "I'm about ready to call it a night."

He quickly crossed the room and placed his

hand over hers. "I thought you were going to trust me."

Yes. She wanted to trust him. But the encounter with Robert Brownley had shaken her, reminding her of how vulnerable trusting made her.

But this was Dwight, not an angry stranger. Dwight, who had loved her so fiercely and held her so tenderly and stayed by her side even when she pushed him away. "He said he wanted to bid on the book. He said he was a collector and he was anxious to complete his collection. He promised to outbid anyone else."

"Did he give you a name?" Dwight asked.

"Robert Brownley."

"I'll try to verify that. So you told him he'd have to bid online or at the auction Saturday?"

"Yes. But he asked to see the book. I told him it was being kept at a secure location— not here. He didn't like that."

"Did he threaten you?" The words were almost a growl.

"No." She smiled weakly, recalling Brown-ley's reaction. "He said that was no way to run a business, or something to that effect—as if that would make me give in to his demands. It was ridiculous, really."

"And then he left?" Dwight asked.

"Then I picked up my phone and told him to leave. I would have dialed nine-one-one if he hadn't headed for the door. I'm sure he knew that."

"He lit out of here fast enough," Dwight said. "I would have stopped him for speeding if I hadn't been concerned about you."

"You didn't have to worry about me." Though she had been relieved to see him when he walked in. "I think he was just a rich busi-nessman who's used to always getting his way. When I dared tell him no, he stormed off in a fit of temper. If he wants the book as badly as he said he did, I'm sure he'll come back Sat-urday."

"If you see him before then, let me know,"

Dwight said. "In the meantime, I'll see what I can find out about him."

"I invited him to the auction reception Friday evening," she said. "I hope he shows up. If he's as wealthy as he appeared to be, and a collector, maybe he'll see a few more items he can't live without."

She closed her laptop and slipped it into her bag. "I'm leaving now. What about you?"

"I'm headed home, too. I'll follow you out to the ranch."

"I really need to find somewhere else to stay," she said as she walked with him out of the museum. "I can't keep imposing on your parents, and it's going to be months before my house can be lived in again."

"My parents are happy to have you." Dwight waited while she locked the door.

"I need my own place."

"Fair enough. But where? Eagle Mountain doesn't have much in the way of affordable rentals. That's why Lacy ended up in your garage apartment, and one reason Maya and Casey are living with Gage."

Brenda thought he would suggest she move in with him and was grateful when he didn't. "It may take me a while to find something," she said. "So I should start looking now."

"Then let me help," he said. "I'll put the word out and let you know if anything comes up. We can put Adelaide to work on it, too. She knows everyone and everything—at least to hear her tell it."

"All right. I'd appreciate that."

Dwight walked her to her car. "Where's your security guard tonight?" he asked.

"I don't know." She looked around, half expecting to see Eddie lurking in the shadows. "I don't know what kind of schedule he and the mayor worked out. They haven't bothered to inform me."

Dwight switched on his flashlight and played the beam over the darkened lot. He stopped with the light shining down the alley. "Isn't that Eddie's Jeep?" he asked. He shifted the light and Brenda gasped at the sight of a figure slumped over the steering wheel.

"Call an ambulance," Dwight said, and took off running for the Jeep.

Chapter Eleven

Dread filled Dwight as he raced toward the Jeep, but when he reached the open driver's-side window he realized Eddie wasn't dead. The figure slumped over the steering wheel snored softly and mumbled when Dwight shook his shoulder. Dwight leaned in closer and spotted a half-eaten pizza on the passenger seat. He sniffed, but didn't smell alcohol—only sausage and pepperoni. He shook the security guard again. "Come on, Eddie, wake up."

But Eddie only leaned sideways, mouth open, snoring away.

"The ambulance is on its way." Brenda joined

him and stared in at Eddie. "Is he drunk?" she asked.

"I don't think so," Dwight said. "I think he's drugged."

"Drugged? By who?"

"I don't know. But he was eating a pizza."

Brenda frowned at the pizza, in its cardboard box with Peggy's Pizza on the front. "Do you think someone put something in his pizza?"

"I think we'd better have it tested, just in case."

"Has anyone else been to the museum—or in the parking lot—in the last half hour or so?" he asked.

"No one's been inside except Mr. Brownley," she said. "When I answered his knock, his was the only vehicle I saw. But why half an hour? Couldn't someone have done this earlier?"

"I'm just guessing, but the pizza is still warm." He frowned at Eddie's slumped figure. "I'll find out from the mayor what time Eddie was supposed to start his shift."

A wailing siren announced the arrival of the ambulance. The paramedics parked and jogged up to the Jeep. "What have we got?" Merrily Rayford, one of the squad's senior paramedics, asked.

Dwight nodded to Eddie. "I think he's been drugged. No idea with what."

She and her partner donned gloves and opened the door of the Jeep. While they examined Eddie, Dwight retrieved an evidence bag from his cruiser and bagged the pizza, box and all. Brenda moved in beside him. "You don't think Parker had anything to do with this, do you?" she asked.

"I don't know what to think," Dwight said. They watched as the paramedics shifted Eddie onto a stretcher.

"His vitals are good," Merrily said. "I don't think he's in any danger, but we'll take him in for a closer look."

"I'll want to question him about what happened," Dwight said.

"From the looks of him, it might be a while," Merrily said. "Maybe in the morning."

"I'll check with the hospital later." He held up the evidence bag. "Meanwhile, I'll get this to the lab."

Brenda waited by her car, arms hugging her stomach, as the ambulance left the lot. "I need to take this in and file a report," Dwight said. "I probably won't be in until late."

She nodded. "Eddie isn't my favorite person, but I hope he's all right."

"I'll let you know." He wanted to kiss her, but settled for squeezing her shoulder. "Go home and try to get some rest. Try not to worry about this."

"It's been so long since I didn't have anything to worry about, I've forgotten what that's like," she said.

THE NEXT MORNING, Dwight and Gage faced a sullen Parker Riddell in the sheriff's department interview room. Gage had picked up the young man at his sister's house, where he and Paige were eating breakfast. Paige had argued against him going to the sheriff's department and had wanted to call a lawyer, but Gage had persuaded her that wasn't necessary. All they wanted was for Parker to answer a few questions. The young man had agreed, as much, Dwight suspected, to get his sister off his back as to placate the cops. He sat now, clothes rumpled and the dark shadow of a beard across his jaw, tattooed forearms crossed over a faded black T-shirt advertising a metal band that had been old when Dwight was a teen.

"I didn't deliver a pizza to Eddie," Parker said in answer to Dwight's first question.

"You were working last night," Dwight said. He had verified this with Peggy at her home earlier this morning.

"Yeah. But I didn't deliver a pizza to that jerk. If he says I did, he's lying."

Eddie wasn't saying anything yet—he was still out of it at the hospital in Montrose. When

Dwight had called to check on him, the nurse on duty had reported that he was sleeping well and not in danger, but they didn't expect him to wake before midmorning.

"He had a pizza from Peggy's on the seat beside him when we found him last night," Dwight said. "He was unconscious."

Parker only looked more sullen. "I don't know anything about that. He must have picked up the pizza at the store."

"Peggy says Eddie didn't pick up a pizza, and he didn't order one delivered, either."

"Then I don't know what to tell you," Parker said.

"Maybe you made up this pizza special and delivered it between your regular orders," Gage said.

"Why would I do that?" Parker's voice rose. "The guy hates me. I wouldn't want to give him a free pizza."

"Maybe you told him it was a peace offering," Dwight suggested. "You were trying to get him to see you aren't a bad guy."

"I don't have any reason to want to impress him."

"What do you know about zolpidem?" Dwight asked.

"It's a sleeping pill, right?"

"So you have heard of it."

He shrugged. "I've heard of lots of things. I mean, I read books, and I watch movies."

"Do you have any zolpidem?" Gage asked. The lab report had come in that morning, showing that the pizza was loaded with the stuff—probably in the form of ground pills sprinkled on top. "Know where to get any?"

"No!" Parker uncrossed his arms and sat up straighter. "I don't have anything to do with drugs anymore. Even when I did, I didn't use downers."

"But they might be a good way to get back at somebody," Gage said. "Load a pizza up with them, put them out of commission for a while."

"Is that what happened to Eddie? I didn't do it. Why would I?"

"Revenge?" Dwight asked. "Or maybe you wanted to break into the museum and didn't want him around."

"I don't want to rob the museum. And it would have been stupid to pull that kind of thing last night—Brenda was working late at the museum."

"How do you know that?" Dwight leaned over him. Was this kid stalking Brenda?

Parker shifted in his chair. "I drove by there on the way to one of my deliveries and saw her car."

Dwight sat back. "I'll bet that disappointed you," he said. "Here you'd gone to all the trouble to make that special pizza for Eddie, and Brenda was foiling your plans."

"No! I told you, I didn't have anything to do with that pizza. Ask Peggy. She would know if I made a pizza."

"She said she left the kitchen to use the bathroom for a few minutes," Dwight said. "You could have slipped in and thrown one together then."

"And she would have noticed if the ingredients were missing. Not to mention it takes more than a few minutes to put together a pizza."

Dwight tried another tack. "When you drove by the museum and saw Brenda's car, did you see Eddie or his truck?"

"No."

"Anyone else?" Gage asked.

"No one else was there—just Brenda's Subaru."

"What time was this?" Dwight asked.

Parker paused, as if considering the question. "I was delivering a Mountain Man special to Mr. Wilbur over on Sixth Street. So that was about seven. A little after."

When Dwight and Brenda found Eddie, it was after nine.

Parker held Dwight's gaze, defiant. "Are you

going to charge me with something, or can I go? I have class this morning."

"You're not being charged with anything." Dwight stood. "We appreciate you coming in for questioning."

Parker said nothing, but left in a hurry. Dwight and Gage returned to Gage's office. "Peggy was pretty insistent that Parker didn't make an extra pizza," Dwight said.

"Her place is pretty small," Gage said. "Even from the bathroom, I think she'd have heard someone messing around in her kitchen."

"She's also positive Eddie didn't order or pick up a pizza," Dwight said.

"Maybe someone else ordered it, added the sleeping pills and took it to Eddie," Gage said. "It's not hard to imagine he's made other enemies."

Dwight grunted in assent. He reviewed their conversation with Parker, searching for any inconsistencies and finding none. "What's a Mountain Man special?" he asked.

"Pork carnitas, green chili and onions," Gage said. "A personal favorite."

Dwight let this pass. "Parker is the most obvious suspect," he said. "But maybe that's just what someone wants us to think."

"Yeah," Gage agreed. "The kid strikes me as smarter than that."

"Drugs can make even smart people do dumb things," Dwight said. "But I think you're right. So, who else had it in for Eddie?"

"Or for Parker," Gage said. "Whoever did this wasn't trying to kill Eddie—just put him out of commission for a while and make it look as if Parker did it."

"So—somebody who wanted to get into the museum?" Dwight shook his head. "Brenda was there until the two of us found Eddie."

"Nobody else was there with her?"

Dwight sat up straight. He'd almost forgotten about Robert Brownley. "A man stopped by to ask about bidding on that book she has up for auction," he said. "He was just leaving when

I showed up—in a black Land Rover. Said his name was Robert Brownley. He wasn't too happy when she told him he couldn't see the book."

"So—before he goes in to see Brenda, he delivers a doctored pizza to Eddie?" Gage shook his head. "Why?"

"To get him out of the way? Maybe he planned to try to take the book if Brenda wouldn't sell it to him."

"I'm definitely going to do a little more checking into Brownley."

"We should be able to interview Eddie in a few hours," Gage said. "Maybe he can solve this whole puzzle."

"Or he'll just throw in another piece that doesn't fit," Dwight said. Every new development only made this case more frustrating.

BRENDA HAD INTENDED to work through lunch the day after her encounter with Robert Brownley and all the excitement with Eddie, but Lacy showed up and insisted she take a break. "You have to eat," Lacy said. Fresh from the hair salon, she looked young and happy—looking at her, Brenda felt old and exhausted.

"I have so much to do," Brenda said, indicating her full desk. "I don't think I can spare the time."

"The work will be here when you get back," Lacy said. "Besides, we need to catch up. We don't see each other as much, now that I'm not living next door."

Brenda did miss her friend. "All right," she said. "You've convinced me."

They walked to Kate's Kitchen on the town's main street. A brisk breeze made a jacket necessary, but the sun shone brightly, and the aspens in people's yards and on the mountainsides above town glowed gold.

"How do you like living at the ranch?" Lacy asked when they were settled into a booth at the café.

"It's very comfortable, but…" Brenda didn't finish the sentence, pretending to study the menu.

"But it's not your place," Lacy said. "You're a guest."

Brenda should have known her friend would understand. "I need to find a place of my own," she said.

"What's the word on your house? Are you going to rebuild?"

"I don't know," she said. "I have a meeting with someone from my insurance company this afternoon. I hope that will give me an idea of how much money I have to work with. I'll probably rebuild, though something different." Something that would be just hers—not the grand house Andy had convinced her she wanted. "Whatever I do, I'll need someplace to live for the foreseeable future. But you know how scarce housing is around here."

"I wasn't thrilled about moving back in with

Mom and Dad, but it's only until the wedding," Lacy said.

"I wondered if you would move in with Travis."

"I considered it, but I guess I'm a little old-fashioned. I want to wait until we're married to live together."

The waitress arrived to take their orders. Brenda opted for the chicken salad, while Lacy chose a burger. As soon as they were alone again, Lacy resumed the conversation.

"Another reason I'm waiting to move in with Travis is that once we're husband and wife, I'll have free rein to redecorate his bachelor pad," she said. She made a face. "It definitely needs some changes."

Brenda thought of Dwight's cabin. There wasn't much about it she would change.

"Dwight has a cabin out at the ranch, doesn't he?" Lacy asked as though reading Brenda's mind. "Have you seen it? What's it like?"

Brenda cursed the blush that heated her face, but she tried to play it cool. "It's really nice," she said. "Comfortable. He has better taste than I expected."

"I'd say he has excellent taste."

Brenda ignored the knowing look in her friend's eyes, and was saved from having to answer by the arrival of their iced teas.

"I'm dying to know the scoop on what happened with Eddie Carstairs," Lacy said. "Travis mentioned he was in the hospital after someone tried to poison him or something. He said you and Dwight found him."

"We found him as we were leaving the museum last night." Brenda added a packet of sweetener to her tea and stirred. "He was slumped over the steering wheel of his Jeep. I thought he was dead."

"That must have given you a turn," Lacy said. "Especially after what happened with Henry Hake."

Brenda shuddered. "Yes. Thankfully, Eddie was just drugged."

"What, did someone shoot a poison dart into him or something?" Lacy asked.

The waitress arrived with their food, her expression not giving any indication that she had heard this alarming question. Brenda crunched a potato chip, then said, "There was a half-eaten pizza on the seat beside him. Dwight sent it to the lab to see if the drugs were in there."

"Ooh, that makes it interesting." She bit into her burger and chewed.

Both women ate silently for a few minutes, then Brenda said, "I think Dwight suspects Parker Riddell." Saying the words out loud made her realize how upset she was by the possibility that Parker—a young man she had grown to like—might be responsible for something so horrible.

"He works at the pizza place, right?" Lacy

asked. "Did he and Eddie have some kind of run-in?"

"You know Eddie," Brenda said. "He likes to throw his weight around."

"And I guess Parker had some trouble with the law before." At Brenda's startled look, Lacy held up her hands. "I'm not gossiping—Paige told me."

"Yes, but he's trying to put that behind him," Brenda said. "He's going to school and working at Peggy's Pizza and volunteering at the museum. I think he's a good guy—and I don't think he hurt Eddie, even though Eddie gave him a really hard time. Parker is trying to make a fresh start." Something she also wanted desperately to do. Not that any of the trouble she had been through was her fault, but she longed to take her life in a different, calmer direction.

"Okay, so why don't you think Parker did it?" Lacy asked.

"He's too smart to do something so obvious,"

Brenda said. "I mean, putting the drugs in a pizza points the finger right at him."

"So you think someone set it up to look like Parker was the guilty party," Lacy said. "But who? And why?"

"I don't know," Brenda said. She stabbed at her salad. "I'm just hoping that for once, it doesn't have anything to do with me or the museum."

"Or maybe whoever doctored the pizza *is* the same person who's been threatening you," Lacy said. "Dwight can arrest him and then you wouldn't have to worry about him anymore."

"Right." She could go back to worrying about her job and where she was going to live. Those were the kinds of problems most people had to solve at one time or another. It had been a while since she had had anything that resembled a "normal" life. She thought she'd welcome the change.

"What you need is a real break," Lacy said. "Why don't we call Paige and Maya and the four of us go out tomorrow night? Dress up, dinner, drinks—just fun. No men, no worries allowed."

"I don't know," Brenda said. "I've got so much to do with the auction and the reception Friday night."

"If I know you, you've already got everything done. If you sit at home tomorrow you'll just fret over all the details you've already gone over a dozen times."

Brenda had to smile at this. "You do know me, don't you?"

"Come on—how about it? We can call it my pre-bachelorette party. Or, I know—we'll say it's an early party for your birthday."

"I don't know," Brenda said. "I'm not much on big celebrations."

"It'll just be four of us. And you need to do something to mark your thirtieth."

Brenda nodded. "All right." She had had her

nose pretty firmly to the grindstone the last few weeks. Maybe a night out was exactly what she needed.

NO GROWN MAN could avoid looking ridiculous in a hospital gown, Dwight decided, as he and Gage entered Eddie Carstairs's hospital room. Eddie, paler than usual, with dark circles under his eyes, pulled the sheet up farther on his chest when he recognized them. "I hope you two have come to get me out of here," he said.

"You'll have to talk to your doctor about that," Gage said. "We're just here to interview you about what happened at the museum last night."

"The doctor was supposed to stop by here an hour ago to sign my discharge papers," Eddie said. "But he's disappeared."

"Then you've got time to talk to us." Dwight

stopped beside the bed, while Gage took up position on the opposite side.

Eddie looked from one to the other of them. "The nurse told me someone tried to kill me with poisoned pizza."

Of course Eddie would go for the most dramatic story first, Dwight thought. "Someone added ground-up sleeping pills to the pizza," he said. "But there wasn't enough there to kill you. It looks like whoever did it wanted to put you out of commission for a while. Who would want to do that, Eddie?"

Eddie looked away. "How should I know?"

"Where did you get the pizza?" Gage asked.

"It was the Tuesday special from Peggy's," he said. "Pepperoni and sausage."

"Peggy says you didn't order a pizza from her last night," Dwight said.

Eddie said nothing.

"Did someone deliver the pizza to you?"

Gage asked. "A friend who knew you were working last night?"

Eddie pressed his lips together, as if holding back words. Then he burst out, "That punk Parker Riddell probably put drugs in the pizza to get back at me," he said.

"Did Parker deliver the pizza to you?" Dwight asked.

Again, Eddie didn't answer right away.

"Do you want us to find who did this or not, Eddie?" Gage asked. "Because we have other things we could be spending our time on than finding out who wanted you to take a long nap."

"Parker didn't deliver the pizza," Eddie said. "But he works at Peggy's. He probably knew it was for me and messed with it."

"Who delivered the pizza?" Dwight asked again, struggling to keep his temper. Gage was right—they had plenty to do without wasting time like this.

"A friend," Eddie said. "But he wouldn't do something like that."

"What is the friend's name?" Dwight asked.

"I don't have to tell you that."

Dwight stared at the man in the bed. "If you know he's innocent, why not give us his name?"

"Because I don't want to."

Dressed in that faded hospital gown, his hair uncombed, mouth set in a stubborn line, Eddie reminded Dwight of an obstinate little kid. He stepped away from the bed. "Call us if you change your mind," he said.

"I'd be careful accepting any more gifts from your friend," Gage said. "Next time, he might decide instead of putting you to sleep, he'll finish you off."

It was possible Eddie went a shade paler beneath the day's growth of beard, but he said nothing as Dwight and Gage left him. They were in Dwight's cruiser before Gage spoke. "Do we know who Eddie's friends are?"

"No. But I'll be asking around." He put the cruiser in gear. "Let's start with the mayor."

"The mayor?"

"He stopped by to talk to Eddie the night Eddie arrested Parker," Dwight said. "Maybe he was there last night, too."

"With a pizza?" Gage asked.

"That's what we're going to find out."

Chapter Twelve

Mayor Larry Rowe's office was so small it scarcely had room for his desk, a filing cabinet and a credenza so covered with piles of paper its surface wasn't visible. When Gage and Dwight entered, he looked up from the screen of a laptop computer, scowling. "What's wrong now?" he barked.

"We just have a few questions for you." Dwight pulled out a chair and sat, while Gage remained standing by the door.

"I don't have time for questions," Larry said, turning his attention back to the computer.

"When was the last time you saw Eddie Carstairs?" Dwight asked.

"I don't know. A few days ago."

"You didn't see him last night?" Dwight asked.

"I went to dinner in Junction with my brother."

"Who's your brother?" Gage asked. "Does he live here?"

"He lives outside of Boston. He's an actor—Garrett Rowe."

Dwight and Gage exchanged glances—neither one of them had ever heard of the mayor's brother. "What time was your dinner?" Dwight asked.

"We left here at five, drove to Junction, had cocktails, then dinner, and lingered, catching up. I don't get to see him that often. I probably got back to my place about midnight."

He swiveled his chair toward them. "Why are you asking these questions?"

"Eddie Carstairs is in the hospital," Dwight

said. "Someone fed him pizza laced with sleeping pills."

Larry made a snorting sound that might have been a laugh. "Eddie never did turn down a meal."

"Do you have any idea who might have given him the pizza?" Gage asked.

"None. Eddie Carstairs is a city employee, not a personal friend."

"Is your brother still in town?" Dwight asked. "We'd like to confirm your story with him."

Larry stiffened. "Are you saying you don't believe me?"

"It's just standard procedure."

"I can give you his number. He's gone back to Boston."

Dwight took the number, and he and Gage left. "What do you think?" Gage asked.

"We'll check with the brother. Not that I think the mayor is really involved, but I don't like to leave loose ends."

As BRENDA PULLED into the drive at her house, her phone pinged with a text from the insurance appraiser, telling her he was running a few minutes late. She sat for a moment, phone still in hand, studying the charred ruins of what had once been her dream home. The stones that had trimmed the foundation stuck up like blackened teeth arranged around a jumble of fallen timbers and empty window frames. She had avoided looking at any of this since the fire, but she was going to have to deal with it sooner rather than later. If nothing else, her neighbors were probably already tired of looking at this eyesore.

She stuffed the phone in her pocket and got out of the car and walked up the stone path to what had been the front door. Everything in the house was a total loss. She still had her laptop and the few clothes she had packed to take to Dwight's parents' home. It didn't matter, she tried to reassure herself. It was all just stuff.

But it was all stuff that she had, for the most part, personally chosen over the years—things it pleased her to look at and to use—the transferware teapot decorated with kittens, the dishes with a pattern of morning glories, the ginger jar bedside lamp with the pale green silk shade. She would miss these little items more than she would grieve the loss of the bedroom furniture and wedding china.

She spotted something glinting in the sunlight and stepped over the threshold and bent down to fish a silver teaspoon from the rubble, blackened, but intact. She found two more nearby, along with the silver top to a teapot and a silver salt cellar—though the walnut buffet that had held them all was a heap of charred wood nearby.

She picked her way across the rooms to the back corner that had been Andy's home office. The fire had started here, and everything in the room had been destroyed, all the little things she kept of her husband's reduced to ash—his desk and chair, a few law books, his university and law school diplomas, his law license. It didn't feel as awful as she would have imagined to lose those things. She supposed she would have eventually put those items away somewhere. They didn't have any children to save them for.

Brakes squealed as a car slowed, and she turned to watch a silver Toyota pull into the driveway and a tall, thin man in khakis and a blue polo unfold himself from the front seat, a folder tucked under one arm. She walked out to meet him. "Alan Treat." He introduced himself and handed her a card, then turned to survey the house. "I understand it was arson," he said.

"That's what the fire department investigator determined, yes."

Treat fixed her with a watery blue eye. "Have they determined who set the fire?" he asked.

"No. Someone has been making anonymous threats. They assume the arsonist was the same person."

His eyebrows were so bushy they looked fake, pasted on like a stage costume. One rose in question and she had a hard time not staring, to see if she could spot the glue. "What has a woman like you done to receive threats?" he asked.

She resented the implication that she had done anything to bring this on herself. "I don't see what any of that has to do with you," she said. "I only want to know what the settlement will be on the house, so that I can make plans."

"We don't pay claims where homeowners burn down their own homes," he said.

"I didn't burn down my own house!" She had raised her voice and glared at him. "I sent a copy of the fire investigator's report to your office. Did you even read it?"

"Most home arson fires are set by the home-owner," he said, his expression bland.

Deputy Defender

"Well, mine wasn't. And if that's all you came to say to me today you can leave, and I will be contacting my attorney."

"Now, now, there's no reason to fly off the handle."

As far as she was concerned, she had every reason to be upset with him, including but not limited to the fact that she absolutely hated being placated with phrases such as "now, now."

"Mr. Treat," she said through clenched teeth, "are you going to discuss the insurance settlement I am entitled to, or not?"

He sighed and opened the folder. He handed her a single sheet of paper. She scanned it until she came to the number at the bottom. She blinked and read it again. "The house was worth far more than this," she said.

"Your settlement is not based on the market value of your home," he said. "It is based on the amount you chose to insure the home for, less your deductible, less the cost of things that weren't destroyed in the fire."

"Everything was destroyed in the fire," she said.

"Not your foundation and the portion of the house below ground level."

She stared at the paper again, trying to make the numbers add up in her head. "I was expecting more," she said.

"Your policy had not been updated in several years," he said. "We do recommend an annual policy review and increased coverage to reflect current market conditions. You are, of course, welcome to appeal, but these things seldom come out in the homeowner's favor."

She looked at the ruins of the home again. "I understand there wasn't a mortgage on the home," Treat continued. "So you will receive a check made out to you, to do with as you wish, though you will, of course, have to pay for cleanup of this lot. I'm sure there is a city ordinance to that effect."

Yes, she would have to pay for cleanup. And then what? She had already considered building a less elaborate home, but would the amount the insurance company was offering be enough?

"If I could have your signature here, we can get the check in the mail to you in a few days." Treat pointed to a blank line at the bottom of the page.

"I don't want to sign anything right now," she said.

Treat closed the folder. "Call us when you're ready." Then he turned, got back in his car and drove away.

When Brenda was sure he was out of sight, she swore and kicked at the front stoop. But that only made her swear more, her toe throbbing. She felt like screaming and throwing things, but had no inclination to provide a free show for neighbors or passing motorists.

A familiar SUV pulled to the curb and Dwight got out. "Are you following me?"

she demanded as he walked toward her, his slightly bowlegged gait so distinctive.

He stopped. "No," he said. "I saw you were here and stopped to talk. Do you want me to leave?"

"No. I'm sorry." She held up the paper, as if in explanation. "The insurance appraiser was here. Mr. Treat. And he wasn't."

"He wasn't a treat?" Dwight started forward again and came to stand beside her.

"No. He was a jerk. He accused me of burning down my own home. And then he offered me this paltry settlement and as much as said it was all my fault for not updating my policy."

Dwight glanced at the paper in her hand, but didn't ask to see it. "Is it enough money to rebuild?" he asked.

"I don't know. I don't think so." She shoved the paper at him. "And he's right—I didn't update the policy. Andy always did those things and I assumed he had purchased replacement coverage. The premium certainly went up every year. I'm mad at Andy all over again for not taking out enough insurance, and angry at myself for not thinking to review the policy once the house was in my name alone. And I'm furious with whoever put me in this position." She glared at the burned-out house. If the arsonist had come along and confessed at that moment, she thought she could have strangled him with her bare hands.

"You've had a rough morning," Dwight said.

"Yes, and you came along at just the wrong time."

"I can take it."

"I don't suppose you're any closer to knowing who did this?" She gestured toward the house.

"I'm sorry, no."

She started back toward her car, and he walked with her. "What are you up to this afternoon?" she asked, making an effort to be more cordial than she felt.

"I'm meeting Gage in a few minutes to head

up to Eagle Mountain Resort. We're supposed to meet a representative of the new owners."

"New owners—already? I mean, Hake's body was only just found." A small shudder went through her at the memory.

"Apparently, these people officially took over only a few days before he disappeared."

"Who are they?"

"Another real estate development company, out of Utah, I think."

"I wonder what they plan to do with the property."

"That's one of the things we're hoping to find out." He held open the car door and returned the settlement statement to her. "What are you doing this afternoon?"

"I'm putting the finishing touches on preparations for the reception tomorrow night and the auction Saturday. Everything is almost in place. Then, tonight, I'm going out with Lacy and Paige and Maya."

"That's a good idea. You've been working

hard—it will be good for you to relax a little." His eyes met hers, so serious and at the same time, tender. "I'm on duty. But call me if you need anything."

"What would I need?" She tried for a flirtatious tone, but wasn't sure she succeeded. "Are you expecting trouble?"

"I didn't mean it that way," he said. "Just that I'm here for you. Whenever."

She waited for the automatic resistance she expected at such a statement, but it didn't come. Instead she felt warmed—comforted by his words. "That's nice to know," she said. "So if I drunk-dial you at two a.m. you won't hang up on me?"

He laughed. "I promise I won't. Though I can't imagine you doing something like that."

"You never know," she said. "I'm beginning to think it's time to try a lot of new things in my life." Maybe even trusting this kind, patient man who was coming to mean so much to her.

DWIGHT TRIED TO put Brenda's troubles out of his mind and focus on work as he and Gage headed out of town toward the Eagle Mountain Resort property. "I talked to the mayor's brother, Garrett, this morning," Dwight said.

"Oh?"

"Yeah. I looked him up online. He actually has quite a few acting credits—dinner theaters, some commercials, some walk-ons in movies. So Larry was telling the truth about that."

"What about their dinner?" Gage asked.

"He confirmed that he met Larry in Junction about six and they were together until after eleven. So the mayor is off the hook."

"Yeah, well, he wasn't at the top of our list anyway," Gage said. "My money is on the guy who was with Brenda—Brownley."

"I haven't been able to find out much about him," Dwight said. "But I'm still looking."

"I ran some more background on these folks we're meeting," Gage said. "Came up with nothing. The company itself—CNG Development—is a subsidiary of a subsidiary of a holding company, and part of a consortium of capital improvement corporations, etc. etc. etc." He waved his hand. "One of these big corporate tangles even the IRS can't figure out, which I guess is the whole point."

"What about the men we're meeting today?" Dwight asked.

"Pierpoint and Reed," Gage said. "Sounds like a law firm. Nothing on them, either. Low-level corporate drones."

Dwight nodded. That was all he'd been able to come up with, as well. "I don't expect to get much out of them," he said. "They'll tell us about as much as a press release, but at least we'll be able to size them up."

"Size them up, and let them know we'll be keeping an eye on them," Gage said.

Marcus Pierpoint and Bryce Reed met the two deputies at the entrance to the property. Dressed in gray business suits and white shirts with no ties, they were cut from the same mold—middle-aged and serious, with firm handshakes and big smiles. Pierpoint was the taller of the two and did most of the talking. Reed tended to echo whatever his colleague said.

"Thanks for meeting with us this afternoon, officers," Pierpoint said after the introductions, as if the meeting had been his idea and not the sheriff's. "We're always interested in establishing good relations with local law enforcement."

"Always good to have the police on our side," Reed agreed.

"What do you know about the activities that have gone on here the past few months?" Dwight asked.

The two businessmen exchanged looks. "You're referring to illegal activities?"

Dwight and Gage said nothing.

"We're aware that wholly unauthorized persons have used the property for illegal activities," Pierpoint said.

"Wholly unauthorized," Reed echoed.

"Did you know any of these persons?" Dwight asked. "Wade Tomlinson or Brock Ryan?"

"No," Pierpoint said, while Reed shook his head.

"What about Henry Hake?" Gage asked.

"What about him?" Pierpoint asked.

"When was the last time you saw him?" Gage asked.

"We never met Mr. Hake," Pierpoint said.

"Do you know anything about his disappearance and subsequent death?" Dwight asked.

"No." Pierpoint shook his head emphatically. "We had nothing to do with any of that." He looked around the property, at the bare limbs of the aspen trees, and the piles of golden leaves among the concrete foundations of buildings that had never been completed. "We were, of course, horrified to learn of the goings-on up here. I assure you both that we intend to put a stop to anything like that."

"Oh?" Dwight waited for Pierpoint to fill in the silence that followed. He struck Dwight as a man who liked to talk.

"We will be installing new gates and locks to keep out trespassers," Pierpoint said. "And we're going to be hiring a security service to patrol the area. We want to make sure every-one knows that this is private property and trespassing will not be tolerated."

"What about the public trail?" Gage asked.

Again the look between the two. "What pub-lic trail?" Pierpoint asked.

"The one on the west side of the property," Gage said. "A court case last year established that it is a public right of way and can't be blocked."

"We contest that assertion and will be ap-pealing," Pierpoint said.

Did the man always talk like he was pre-senting a case in court? Dwight wondered.

"Until the court order is overturned, any gates or locks you install blocking the trail will be removed," Dwight said.

Pierpoint's expression made it clear he didn't like this, but wisely didn't argue.

"What are your plans for the property?" Gage asked.

"We will be building a private research facility on-site," Pierpoint said.

"What kind of research?" Dwight asked.

"We're not at liberty to say, but the remote location and high altitude could prove beneficial," Pierpoint said.

"Was the laboratory we found here on the property, in the underground bunker, yours?" Dwight asked.

"No," Pierpoint said. "That has nothing to do with us. We'll be building a completely modern, state-of-the-art facility."

"You'll be applying for all the proper permits from the county," Gage said.

"Of course." Reed apparently decided it was time for him to get another word in.

"Is there anything else we can do for you?" Pierpoint asked. He pulled a set of car keys from his pocket. "We have another meeting we need to get to."

"That's all for now," Dwight said.

He and Gage returned to Dwight's SUV. Pierpoint and Reed followed and Reed shut and locked the gate behind them. Dwight waited until he was on the road again before he spoke. "What do you think?" he asked Gage.

"Hard to say if they were telling the truth or not," Gage said. "I can't think of any good reason they would be linked to Henry Hake's disappearance and death—the transfer of the property was completed before he died. And it doesn't make sense they would have a connection to Wade and Brock." He shrugged. "But stranger things have happened."

"Interesting that they're going to use the place for a research facility," Dwight said.

"I don't know," Gage said. "I think high-altitude research is kind of a thing these days. There are a couple of facilities around Denver—and one in Crested Butte—studying climate and who knows what else."

Dwight nodded. "I guess so. Just seems like a remote place to do research."

"Maybe the remote location is an advantage," Gage said. He shifted in his seat. "The environmental folks might like that idea better than a big resort."

"Maybe. And the place is an eyesore in the condition it's in now."

"Do you really think they had no idea what was going on up there?" Gage asked. "I mean, that underground lab, what happened with me and Maya—and don't forget someone shot at me and at Travis on different occasions. It was like they were using that place as a headquarters for something."

"These guys are based in Utah," Dwight said. "I can see how they might not know if someone was up to something on the place. And I can see how it would attract the wrong element—all those empty buildings and the remote location. I'm glad they're going to be looking after the place now."

"That public trail is going to be a sticking point. If they try to close it, Paige and her group will fight them on it."

"Let's hope we don't have to get involved," Dwight said. "I'd be happy if I never had to go up to Eagle Mountain Resort again."

Chapter Thirteen

It didn't take long for the four women to agree that a proper night out on the town meant a town other than Eagle Mountain. "There's only one bar there, there's no place to dance, the only fancy places to eat are full of tourists, and everyone we know will see us and gossip about every move we make." Paige ticked off all the reasons the quartet had to leave town if they were really going to cut loose.

"Just how wild do you plan on this evening being?" Maya asked. A recent transplant from Denver, the high school teacher with dip-dyed blue hair probably had more party girl experience than any of them.

"I don't know," Lacy said. "Do you think we can get enough drinks in Brenda that she'll dance on a table?"

"It will never happen," Brenda said. "You know I don't drink that much. And someone has to stay sober enough to drive."

"I've already taken care of that," Lacy said. "No worries about any of us getting behind the wheel with too much to drink."

"What do you mean?" Paige asked, clearly skeptical.

"We have a driver." She gestured to the window and the street outside her parents' house. A young man dressed in jeans, a navy blazer, and a chauffeur's cap saw them all peering at him and tipped his hat.

"Parker!" Paige exclaimed.

"He had the night off, he doesn't drink as a condition of his parole, and he's a good driver," Lacy said. "I figure it would be the perfect solution."

"I'm not sure how I feel about going out with my kid brother," Paige said as the women gathered their purses and wraps and headed for the door.

"He's not going to go into the restaurant or club with us," Lacy said. "And I've already told him that if he tries to take any photographs of any of us in compromising positions, I'll take his phone and step on it." She extended one foot to display a wicked-looking stiletto heel. "I think he believed me."

Parker drove them to Junction, a college town about an hour away, in the dark blue Toyota sedan he usually used for pizza delivery. Paige had made the dinner reservations, selecting a Japanese grill where they sat on cushions around a low table while a chef made their meals to order—and flirted outrageously. They took turns daring one another to eat unfamiliar foods—they all tried the octopus, but

Paige was the only one who would brave eating eel.

By her second glass of wine, Brenda realized she had laughed more in the last hour than she probably had in the last year. While a waitress cleared away their dinner plates, she excused herself to use the ladies' room.

"I'll go, too," Lacy said, and hurried after her.

"Thank you for pulling this together," Brenda said when the two friends found themselves alone in the ladies' room. "You were right—this is exactly what I needed."

"It's what I needed, too," Lacy said. "I've been working so hard at school and on plans for the wedding—it feels great to relax with friends. As much as I love Travis, being with him isn't the same as being with female friends, you know?"

Brenda nodded, too choked up to speak. In the months following Andy's death, she had too often cut herself off from others. Only recently had friends like Lacy reminded her how important other people were in her life.

A few moments later, they emerged from the restroom into the hallway that divided the restaurant into two halves—their table was in a large space full of low tables, colorful cushions, shoji screens and traditional Japanese décor. The other side of the restaurant had a more Western vibe, with dark booths and small tables.

Brenda glanced into this space and stopped short.

"What is it?" Lacy asked.

Brenda took a step back, behind a large potted firm. "That booth on the far side of the room—the second one from the left." She kept her voice low, just above a whisper. "Is that Eddie Carstairs?"

Lacy peered around the firm. "It is him! But who is he with?"

The two women stared between the fronds of the fern at Eddie, who was dressed in a dark suit a little too big for his slight frame, and at the man across from him. This man also wore a dark suit, though better tailored and obviously more expensive than Eddie's. His upper face was in shadow, only his chin visible. "I can't tell who that is," Brenda said.

"Eddie looks upset about something," Lacy said. At that moment, Eddie leaned forward, jaw set, and stabbed his finger at the man opposite. The man didn't even flinch, merely waited for Eddie to finish whatever he was saying.

Brenda tugged on Lacy's arm. "It doesn't matter. Let's get out of here before he sees us." Having to deal with Eddie would definitely put a damper on the night.

"What do you think Eddie is doing here?" Lacy asked.

Brenda shook her head. "I don't know. Maybe his brother is in town. Or a friend from college or a cousin. Or maybe it's a business meeting." The more she thought about the scene at the table, the more it struck her that way—very businesslike. Or maybe it was just that the other man seemed like a businessman to her—the tailored suit, the stoic demeanor.

"I told them to go ahead and bring our checks," Paige said when Brenda and Lacy returned to the table.

"What's next on the agenda?" Brenda asked as she fished her wallet out of her purse.

"We're going to a great club a friend told me about," Maya said. "They have a fantastic DJ and a big dance floor. Plenty of room for the four of us to get out there and show our stuff." She laughed at what must have been the expression on Brenda's face. "It's okay to dance without men, you know," she said. "Women do it all the time at places like this."

"Sure," Brenda said. "It sounds like fun." Though she couldn't help feeling a little pang of nostalgia for the times she and Andy had danced arm in arm. For all his faults, he had been a great dancer.

They paid their bills, then gathered their belongings and filed out of the dining room. Brenda and Lacy waited while Maya and Paige went to the ladies' room. They were standing in the foyer when two men emerged from the other side of the restaurant and almost collided with them. "What are you doing here?" Eddie demanded. He glared at Brenda, face flushed.

"We're having dinner," Brenda said. "The same as you." She glanced behind him, toward his companion, but the other man was already gone. She'd been so focused on Eddie, she had never gotten a good look at him.

"You must be feeling better," Lacy said. "Have they caught whoever it was who tried to poison you?"

"It wasn't poison," Eddie said. He glared at the two women. "I have to go." Then he turned and hurried out the door.

"Was that Eddie Carstairs?" Paige joined them, Maya close behind.

"Yes," Lacy said. "He apparently decided to have dinner here, too."

"I guess he won't want pizza for a long time." Maya covered her mouth and giggled. "I'm sorry, that was probably mean."

"He wasn't happy to see us, that's for sure," Brenda said. The women trooped out to the parking lot, where Parker met them at the car. He had opted to go across the street to a popular burger place for dinner.

"How was your dinner?" Brenda asked as he unlocked the car for them.

"Good. I met a couple of cute girls." He grinned. "One of them gave me her number."

"Since when are you such a flirt?" Paige asked.

"You should try it sometime, sis," he said. "It's fun."

"Oh no!"

At the cry from the rear of the car, the others turned to find Maya staring down at the rear wheel. She looked up at them, dismayed. "We've got a flat."

"Let me see." Parker moved to her side and knelt to check the tire, which was, indeed, deflated.

"You have a spare, right?" Paige asked.

Parker stood and walked around the rear of the car to the other side. "I have one spare," he said. "But both rear tires are flat."

"Did we run over nails or something?" Lacy looked around, as if expecting to find the cause of the tire damage nearby.

"Or something." Parker turned to Paige. "Maybe you'd better call the cops."

"Why?" she asked, even as she pulled out her phone.

"We didn't run over anything," Parker said. "Both tires have been slashed."

"EDDIE'S THE OBVIOUS suspect for slashing the tires, but he denies everything," Dwight said when he saw Brenda the next night before the museum reception. Whereas when she had called last night to tell him about the incident in the restaurant parking lot she had been clearly upset, tonight she was the picture of calm, in an ankle-length midnight-blue dress that bared her shoulders and clung to her curves, subtle silver threads shimmering with every movement. She wore her blond hair piled on top of her head, delicate tendrils framing her face. The overall effect was elegant and incredibly sexy.

He had traded in his uniform for a dark gray Western-cut suit and polished python boots, though he was technically on the job, his service weapon in a holster beneath the jacket. Travis and Gage were in attendance as well, to beef up the security provided by Eddie. They would keep an eye on the valuable auction items, but Dwight's main focus was on protecting Brenda.

"I don't think Eddie did it," she said. "I don't see how he would have had time. We were talking to him in the lobby of the restaurant right up until we walked out to the car."

"What about his friend?" Dwight asked. "The man he was having dinner with. You said he left the restaurant ahead of Eddie."

"Maybe." She frowned. "But why? Neither Lacy nor I recognized him. We really didn't get a good look at him. His face was in shadow in the restaurant."

"I wish you had seen him. I'd love to know who he is."

"Do you think he's the same person who brought Eddie the doctored pizza?" she asked.

"Maybe." Dwight had already considered this—whoever had dosed that pizza with sleeping pills had been someone Eddie either wanted to protect, or didn't want to admit to knowing. "But then, why would Eddie go out to dinner with him a few nights later?"

"Maybe Eddie set up the meeting to confront the guy about the pizza. He wanted to do it away from Eagle Mountain, where someone might see them together. That would explain why he was so upset to run into us."

"Maybe." He looked around the crowd. At least eighty people were in attendance, drifting through the rooms of the museum, sipping cocktails and nibbling canapés, admiring the items on display and checking out the auction items arrayed on tables in the front rooms. Attire ranged from business suits and cocktail dresses to jeans and T-shirts. He didn't recognize a dozen or more of the guests, though he spotted the mayor across the room, in conversation with the woman who headed up the local beautification committee. "Is Robert Brownley here?" he asked.

"I haven't seen him. Why?"

"I tried to find out some background information on him, but I couldn't come up with anything."

"I did an online search, too," she admitted. "But nothing I came up with sounded like him.

But if he's as wealthy as he seemed, maybe he purposely keeps a low profile."

"Maybe." There were too many maybes involved in this case.

"Oh look, there's Professor Gibson." She touched Dwight's arm. "Excuse me, I want to speak to him."

"Of course." Dwight watched her cross the room and greet the professor. She smiled at the older man, and Dwight felt a now-familiar catch in his chest. He would never get tired of looking at that smile, of watching the play of emotions on her face. He could imagine himself looking at her this way when they were both twenty or forty or sixty years older. The problem was—how could he persuade her to see that kind of future? She had been hurt so much in the past, he had the sense that she was afraid to look too far ahead.

Patience, he told himself. That was the key to dealing with Brenda—and the key to investigating any case. He went to join Travis by the auction display. The sheriff wore a black Western jacket, black jeans and a black Stetson, with a white shirt and string tie. Lacy, in a sleeveless red cocktail dress trimmed with fringe, stood beside him. They made a striking couple.

"Hello, Lacy." Dwight touched the brim of his hat and nodded to her.

"Don't you look handsome." She turned to Travis. "All of you clean up so well."

Travis's answer was a grunt. Lacy laughed. "You'd rather be in uniform, wouldn't you?" She kissed his cheek. "Dwight has a look in his eye like he wants to talk shop, so I'm going to visit with Paige." She smiled at Dwight and left them.

"Anyone particularly interested in the book?" Dwight asked.

"Nope." Travis glanced toward where the book sat on a raised platform in the very center of the table to their left. "A couple of people have looked at it, but no one has lingered."

He shifted toward his deputy. "How's Brenda doing?"

"She seems calm. I think the whole episode with the tire annoyed her more than it frightened her."

Travis nodded. "She doesn't frighten easily."

"She said Robert Brownley hasn't shown up."

"Anybody else here who shouldn't be?"

"Brenda didn't mention anyone." Laughter rose from a knot of people near the door to the hallway and he turned to look toward them. "There are quite a few people from out of town."

"Let's hope they bid high and the museum makes some money," Travis said. He looked toward the auction items again. "Lacy has her heart set on that quilt. I put in a bid on it— thought it might make a good wedding present."

"I imagine it would." This brought to mind the question of what *he* should give the happy couple as a gift—something that hadn't occurred to him until this moment.

Fortunately, he didn't have to wrestle with this question for long. The arrival of Eddie Carstairs interrupted him. Unlike the dressed-up sheriff and deputies, he wore khaki pants and shirt that looked very much like the Rayford County Sheriff's Department uniforms, though in place of the sheriff's department patch, his shirt had a dark blue star with the word *Security* embroidered in gold lettering across it. "What are you two doing hovering around the auction items?" Eddie asked.

"Just keeping an eye on them," Travis said.

"That's my job." Eddie rested his hand at his hip, very near the holster for a pistol. He had a permit for the weapon, and his sheriff's department training would have ensured he knew how to use it safely, but the sight of it still made Dwight uncomfortable. Maybe that was behind Dwight's decision to make Eddie uncomfortable in turn.

"Who were you having dinner with last night?" Dwight asked.

Eddie's cheeks flushed. "We already went over all that," he said. "It's none of your business."

"It's my business if he slashed the tires on the car Brenda and her friends were in." Dwight could feel Travis's steady gaze on him. Was the sheriff going to reprimand him for interrogating a witness in a public place like this? Or was Travis merely waiting to see what Eddie would say?

"Maybe Parker slashed the tires himself to make me look bad," Eddie said. "Did you ever think of that?"

Dwight looked over Eddie's shoulder to where Parker Riddell, in black pants and a white long-sleeved shirt that hid his many tattoos, offered a group of silver-haired women a tray of bacon-wrapped shrimp. He had considered the idea that Parker had slashed the tires, either to frighten the women or to call attention to himself for some reason. But everything he had learned from the people who knew and worked with him confirmed that Parker was staying on the straight and narrow. Brenda certainly thought so, and her opinion carried more and more weight with Dwight.

"What is he doing here, anyway?" Eddie asked. "He doesn't have any business being around all these valuable items. If anything disappears, he's my number one suspect."

Travis and Dwight both ignored the comment. Dwight could almost hear Eddie's teeth grinding in frustration at his failure to elicit a response.

"Who is that man Brenda is talking to?" Eddie asked.

Dwight followed Eddie's gaze to where Brenda stood with Professor Gibson, their heads inclined toward each other, deep in conversation. He was tempted to tell Eddie the man's identity was none of his business, but Travis answered, "That's Professor Gibson.

He owned that book—*The Secret History of Rayford County*—before Andy Stenson got hold of it."

Eddie studied the couple. "He and Brenda certainly look cozy," he said. He turned to Dwight. "You might have some competition, Prentice."

Dwight glared at him. He could either deny anything was going on between him and Brenda—which would be a lie—or remain silent and confirm Eddie's suspicions. The man was a worse gossip than Adelaide, and in Eddie's case, Dwight always had the sense Eddie was searching for any scrap of information he could use to his own advantage. He decided to play it cool. "I wasn't aware we were running a race. Excuse me. I see someone I'd like to speak with." The mayor had just entered the room, and as long as he was here, Dwight wanted to find out where Brenda's boss—and Eddie's, for that matter—had been when Brenda's tires were being slashed.

"Professor, I'd like you to meet Parker Riddell. He's one of my best volunteers—and he's studying history at the community college." Brenda had waylaid the young man as he hurried past with yet another tray or hors d'oeuvres.

"Always good to meet a young person who's interested in history." Professor Gibson offered his hand. "Is there a particular period you'd like to focus on?"

Parker shifted the serving tray and shook the professor's hand. "I'm not sure, sir. American history. The West. And I'm really interested in World War II."

Gibson nodded and asked a few more questions about the classes Parker was currently enrolled in, and made some recommendations of books he should read. "History isn't the most lucrative field these days," he said. "But it can be a very rewarding one."

"I hope so, sir." Parker shifted the tray again.

"I'd better go pass these out before they get cold. It was nice to meet you."

"Nice to meet you, too, young man."

When Parker had left them, the professor turned back to Brenda. "You've done a wonderful job with this place," he said. "It's a real gem."

"We think so," Brenda said. Now seemed as good a time as any to bring up what was, after all, an awkward subject. "I want to thank you for being so understanding about *The Secret History of Rayford County, Colorado*. I truly had no idea my late husband had borrowed it from you when I listed it for auction."

"If I thought you had, I might not have been so understanding," Gibson said. "As it is, proving my claim would have been difficult, and I'm pleased to have the sale go to support a worthy cause. I'm curious, though—did you read the book?"

"I did. More than once. And I made quite a few notes."

He nodded. "At one time I tried very hard to determine where the secret lab might have been located. My theory is the government destroyed it once the project ended. Otherwise someone would have found it by now."

"The sheriff's department found what looked like a laboratory up at Eagle Mountain Resort, but it apparently wasn't nearly old enough to have been used during the war."

"Government documents are being declassified all the time," Gibson said. "I imagine before too many more years, someone will find out the location. In the meantime, that book attracts attention from everyone from conspiracy theorists to serious collectors. I hope it brings a high price to help support the museum."

She looked around, past the well-dressed guests to the photos and displays on the walls. To many people, the items in these rooms were just old junk, relics of a time long past. But to Brenda and other history lovers, they were links to the past—a look at how the people who had settled this part of the country had once lived. She believed those people still had lessons to teach. "I love this place," she said. "And I'm determined to do everything I can to keep it going."

"I have some ideas about that I'd love to talk to you about," the professor said. "I know—"

But a terrified scream cut off his words and silenced the conversations of those around them. A man Brenda didn't know, face blanched paper-white, staggered into the room. "Upstairs...a body...hanging," he gasped.

Chapter Fourteen

Dwight pushed through the crowd toward the stairs, Travis close behind him. "Police! Let us through!" he shouted, over the panicked voices of those rushing down the narrow staircase. Men and women turned sideways to let him pass, their frightened faces a blur as he mounted the steps two at a time. At the top, he paused and looked around.

"In there!" A man motioned toward a room to the left. Travis moved up beside Dwight, his gun drawn. "You take right. I'll go in on the left."

Dwight nodded. They had no reason to believe anyone dangerous was inside the room, but best to be prepared. Heart hammering, he moved to the right side of the door. Travis positioned himself across from him. At his nod, they went in, guns drawn.

Dwight's breath caught as he came face-to-face with a man in white—then he felt foolish, and a little shaky, as he realized the figure was actually a mannequin in a World War II sailor's uniform. He scanned the rest of the room, which was filled with old military paraphernalia, from helmets and maps to a Vietnam-era field radio and navy semaphore flags.

The body hung from the ceiling in the corner, positioned so that someone had to enter the room to see it. In the dimmer light in that part of the room, it did indeed look human—but closer inspection revealed that this, too, was a mannequin, dressed in the olive drab of a World War II-era sergeant.

Travis holstered his weapon. "Someone's idea of a sick joke," he said.

"What is it? Someone said there was a body?"

Eddie, red-faced and out of breath, appeared behind them, his gun drawn.

"Put that weapon away," Travis barked. "And go back downstairs."

Eddie holstered the gun, but made no move to leave. "I'm the security guard for the museum," he said. "I need to know what's going on."

"Nothing's going on," Dwight said. He gestured to the hanging mannequin. "Some joker decided to play a prank."

Eddie started to approach the mannequin, but Travis waved him back. "Stay out of the crime scene," he ordered.

Eddie laughed. "Crime scene? It's a mannequin."

"Someone wanted to frighten the people here tonight," Travis said. "I want to know who."

Brenda appeared behind Eddie in the doorway to the room, looking pale but determined. "What is going on?" she asked.

"Someone hung one of your mannequins from a ceiling beam," Travis said. "Then someone looked in, thought it was a body in the dim light and panicked."

Brenda moved into the room and looked toward the mannequin in the corner. She shuddered. "It certainly does look like a body from here. Who would do such a thing?"

"Where have you been, Eddie?" Dwight asked.

"Are you accusing me of doing something like this? I've been working, protecting the visitors to the museum and the museum's valuable property."

Dwight didn't let his disdain show on his face. Eddie acted as if he had personally been guarding every exhibit.

"The auction items!" Brenda's eyes widened and she started to turn away.

"Gage is guarding them," Travis said.

Dwight nodded. "You thought this might be a distraction—get us all up here and the thief could help himself to whatever he liked downstairs."

"It was a possibility." Travis looked up at the dangling mannequin. "Let's close off this room until we can get a crime scene team in to take a look. And we'll need to talk to whoever was up here when it was discovered."

"Some people have already left," Brenda said. "I think we can safely say this has put a damper on the evening." She turned around to look toward the hallway. "There have been dozens of people in and out of these rooms all night. How could someone do this without being seen?"

Dwight studied the layout of the room. "You can't see this corner from the hallway," he said. "If our prankster had the rope handy, he could wait until he was alone in here and loop it around the mannequin's neck. Throw the rope over the beam, hoist up the mannequin, secure the rope and stroll out. It might take less than a minute."

"You can ask if anyone saw anything," Brenda said. "Maybe you'll get lucky."

"Maybe." Travis didn't sound convinced.

"Do you have a guest list or anything with the names of everyone who attended tonight?" Dwight asked.

"There's a guest book—but whether or not people signed it was up to them."

"Let's go get it."

He descended the stairs right behind her, and a crowd of people surrounded them, firing questions—most versions of "What happened?"

"False alarm," he said, one hand at Brenda's back. He leaned closer to whisper in her ear, the floral scent of her perfume momentarily distracting him, but he forced his attention back to the task at hand. "You'd better make an announcement and send them home."

She nodded and climbed back up a few steps until she was above the crowd. Everyone fell silent. "Thank you all so much for coming tonight," she said. "I hope we see all of you at the auction tomorrow morning. You'll be able to get another look at all the items available tomorrow starting at nine a.m. See you then."

Eddie had appeared on the stairs behind Brenda as she spoke. As he came down after her, Dwight snagged his arm. "Help herd everyone out the door," he said.

Eddie opened his mouth as if to argue, but apparently thought better of it. He nodded and moved on, murmuring, "Good night," and, "Thank you for coming," as he urged people toward the open front doors.

"I want to check with Gage that the auction items are all right," Brenda said to Dwight.

"Good idea." They fought their way against the flow of the crowd to the next room, where Gage stood between the tables of auction items. "Any problems?" Dwight asked.

"Everything is still here, and I didn't notice anyone paying particular attention to me or the merchandise," Gage said. "What happened up there?"

"Someone hung a mannequin from a ceiling beam," Dwight said, keeping his voice low, though only a few people remained, waiting for their turn to exit.

"Sick joke," Gage said.

"Maybe," Dwight said.

"Eddie is supposed to be on duty all night," Brenda said. "But I'd feel better if one of you would take the book back to the station and lock it in the safe until morning." She picked up *The Secret History of Rayford County, Colorado.* "It's by far our most valuable item."

"I'll make sure it's safe." Dwight took the book from her. Gone was the sparkling, happy woman of earlier in the evening. She looked exhausted, weighed down by worry. "We don't know that the hung mannequin had anything to do with the book," he said.

"No, but too many unsettling things have

been happening." She looked around the room. "I need to get you that guest book."

He followed her back to the entry hall, where they found Lacy with Travis. "Do you need me to stay and help with anything?" Lacy asked.

"No, thank you," Brenda said. "I'm going to go in a few minutes myself."

"We'll be here a little while longer," Travis said. "We'll lock up when we leave, and we'll be back in the morning for the auction."

"So will I." Lacy squeezed Brenda's shoulder. "Are you okay?"

Brenda nodded. "I'm fine."

Lacy frowned, but didn't say anything else. "I'll walk you to your car," Travis said, and they headed out the door.

"The guest book is over here," Brenda said, walking to a small desk to the right of the door. The guest book, bound in blue leather, lay open on the top, a brass can filled with pens next to it. Signatures half filled the open page. Brenda picked up the book and flipped through it. "I don't see Robert Brownley's name here," she said. "And I didn't see him among the guests. Maybe he changed his mind about bidding for the book."

"Or maybe, since he plans to outbid everyone else, he'll be here tomorrow." Dwight slid the book from her hand, closed it and tucked it under his arm. He stroked her cheek. "Are you okay?"

She sighed. "I'm ready for all this to be over." She shook her head. "I don't know why that stupid mannequin upset me so much. It's just a sick joke, like Gage said. But it took me back to when we found Henry Hake..."

Her voice trailed away. Dwight set the book on the desk once more and pulled her to him. She rested her head on his shoulder, and he held her tightly for a long moment, saying nothing. He closed his eyes and let himself revel in the sweet scent and soft feel of her. When all this was over, he'd ask her to go away with him somewhere—a beach where they could lie side by side on the sand and sip fruity drinks. He smiled, picturing Brenda in a bikini.

"What are you smiling about?" She pushed away from him.

"How did you know I was smiling?" he asked, his expression solemn once more.

"I felt it." She rested a hand on his chest.

"I'll tell you later," he said. "Now, go home and get some rest. I'll take care of everything here."

She looked past him, at the crime scene techs filing up the stairs. "I feel like I should stay."

"There's nothing you can do. Go home and rest."

"All right. Let me get my purse." He waited while she retrieved her purse from her office, then walked with her to her car.

"We'll talk in the morning," he said. "Try not to worry."

She nodded. "I'm not going to let a stupid prank get the best of me." She rose on tiptoe to kiss his cheek. "I was thinking...instead of going to the ranch house, I might wait for you at your cabin."

The words sent a current of heat through him. "I'd like that." He fished his key from his pocket and pressed it into her palm. "You'll need this."

"Try not to be too late."

No, he'd be wrapping up his business here as quickly as possible. One lifeless mannequin couldn't compete with the very live woman he would have waiting for him.

At least her bold suggestion to Dwight had provided a welcome distraction from the terrible way the evening had ended, Brenda thought as she drove through town. When he had pulled her to him and held her—just held her, without offering empty words or advice—she had felt so comforted and *supported*. He wasn't hovering or trying to control her or dismiss her or any of the things she had experienced at the hands of other men. Dwight was simply there for her, letting her find her own strength by lending her some of his. His calm, practical nature was exactly what she needed.

But Dwight was more than a calming presence or a strong friend. He was a man she wanted to be with more and more. Time to stop denying that and admit what was happening. In spite of all her efforts to resist—all the *logical* reasons this shouldn't be happening—Brenda had fallen in love with Dwight. The realization made her a little light-headed.

Maybe, when things had calmed down—after the auction at least—she would find a way to tell him.

That is, if she could get through the auction with no more disasters. At least it hadn't been a real body hanging in the display room, but who would do something like that? Was someone trying to frighten her?

Everyone in Eagle Mountain—and anyone who read the local newspaper—would have known that she and Dwight had found Henry Hake hanging in that underground laboratory at Eagle Mountain Resort. Was that mannequin supposed to be a sick reminder of that event—or some kind of warning?

She rubbed her temple, trying to ward off the headache that was building there. It didn't make sense, but then, nothing that had happened really did. She went over all the events in her mind—the two threatening notes on cheery yellow stationery, the crime scene photo from Andy's murder, the stolen banner announcing the auction, the fire that had destroyed her house, the slashed tires on the car that had been transporting her and her friends—and now this hanging mannequin. It was such a crazy combination of shocking violence and almost juvenile pranks. Everything seemed to have been aimed at either her or the museum, but why?

She turned onto the county road that led from town up to the Prentices' ranch. She couldn't keep from going over the events in her mind. It was like trying to find a missing piece in a jigsaw puzzle—find that piece, that link, and everything would make sense. She would have a clear picture where there had been only chaos before.

Glaring lights filled the car, reflecting off the rearview mirror and into her eyes as a vehicle with its brights on came up behind her. Brenda put up a hand to shield her eyes from the glare and stepped on the brakes. She pulled the Subaru toward the shoulder, hoping the rude person behind her would pass. The car—or probably a truck, judging by the height of the headlights—was approaching very fast, obviously in a hurry to get somewhere. She would have pulled off the road altogether, but there wasn't room. The Eagle River followed the road here, the waters spilling over rocks some ten feet below.

She shifted her gaze to her side mirror and realized the other driver wasn't slowing down.

He was traveling much too fast for this narrow, winding road. She took her foot off the brake and sped up, thinking she should drive until there was a safe place to pull over. But she had no time to gain much speed before the other vehicle was on her. Horrified, she realized the other driver wasn't going to stop. He hit her full-on, throwing her forward, her airbag exploding with painful violence, the car skidding off the pavement, rocketing down the bank of the river and into the icy water.

Chapter Fifteen

Pain throbbed in Brenda's head, and her chest hurt. She moaned and tried to shift into a more comfortable position, held upright by her seat belt. Confused, she opened her eyes and stared through the spiderwebbed windshield into a tangle of broken tree limbs and underbrush illuminated by one headlight. The lights on the dash bathed the interior of the car in a faint blue glow. The airbags had deflated, though their powdery residue lay like a dusting of sugar over everything. As her still-painful head began to clear, Brenda realized the car was still running. She felt around on the steering column and found the key, and turned it to cut the motor.

She had expected silence, but instead heard a car door slam and someone approaching, clumsy footsteps slipping and sliding on the steep embankment down from the road. The memory of the bright headlights rushing toward her sent panic through her, and she grappled to unfasten the seat belt. If her attacker was coming after her, she would have to run, to hide—

She was still fumbling with the seat belt when her door was wrenched open. A tall, dark figure, face covered by a black ski mask, grabbed her arm and shook her. "Give it to me!" he demanded, in a gruff, unfamiliar voice.

"G-give you what?" Brenda stared up at him, fighting for calm. She had to think, but her head hurt so much—the pain made her nauseous.

"Give me the book!"

The book. She wished she had never laid eyes on that cursed book. "I don't have it," she said.

"It's not at the museum. Where is it?"

"The sheriff has it."

Her attacker let loose a stream of invective that had her shrinking back. But even as she did so, she put her right hand down by her side, on the button to release the seat belt. As soon as she saw her chance, she would leap from the car and run. Better to risk the dangers of the mountainside than this madman.

"You're lying!" He punctuated this statement by thrusting a pistol in her face. Brenda had seen plenty of firearms in her life. Her father had collected guns. The museum owned several antique pistols and rifles. But she had never been eye to eye with a weapon that was pointed directly at her. She was both terrified and icily calm.

"I'm not lying," she said, shocked by how even her voice sounded. It was almost as if some other person—a cooler, more coura-geous person—had taken over her body. "The sheriff has the book."

"Give me your purse." He thrust the gun to-ward her.

"It's in the passenger seat," she said. "You're welcome to it."

He reached past her and grabbed the purse, as well as the tote bag that contained auction paperwork she had planned to look over be-fore she returned to work in the morning. He riffled through these items, then tossed them onto the ground at his feet. She bit her tongue to keep from pointing out that she had al-ready told him she didn't have the book. Why wouldn't he believe her?

"Where were you going tonight?" he asked, the end of the barrel of the gun only a few inches from her forehead.

"I was going home," she said.

"You don't live out this way," he said.

I didn't until you burned down my house,

she thought. But then, maybe this man hadn't burned her house. She had no way of knowing. "I'm staying with friends," she said.

"Friends? Or one particular friend?" He reached over and unsnapped the seat belt, then dragged her from the car. "You're staying with that cop, aren't you? The tall, dark-haired one."

Brenda said nothing.

"He lives on a ranch, doesn't he?" the man asked. When she didn't answer, he yanked on her arm—hard.

She cried out and tried to pull away, but he only held on tighter and dragged her after him. "Come on," he said.

"Where are you taking me?" she asked.

"To wait for your boyfriend."

WRAPPING THINGS UP at the museum took longer than Dwight had wanted. Usually, he appreciated how methodical and thorough Travis could be, but tonight the routine had chafed. Brenda was waiting, and Dwight didn't want to lose the chance to be with her—not just to make love, though he certainly hoped they would do that, but to talk to her about something besides the case. About their future.

Finally, he had gotten away, with a reminder from Travis that he would need a report on his desk in the morning. Dwight had suppressed a groan and nodded, then hurried away, leaving Travis and Gage to lock up the museum. He pushed the SUV on the drive to the ranch, though the narrow, curvy road limited how fast he could safely travel. He watched the sides of the road for deer or elk that might decide to leap out in front of him. He had attended more than one wreck caused by wildlife. Most of the people involved escaped with only minor damage, but he still remembered one young woman who had been killed when her truck rolled down the embankment, crushing her, after she swerved to avoid a deer.

His headlights glanced off a vehicle parked ahead, half on the shoulder, half in his lane, and he braked. The car appeared empty, not running. Had someone abandoned it like this? He prepared to pull in behind it. He might have to call a tow truck to retrieve the big SUV—another delay, but necessary. Parked as it was, the vehicle was a real hazard.

But as he pulled in behind the SUV, two figures emerged ahead of the vehicle, climbing up from the stream bank. The larger figure—a man—appeared to be dragging the smaller one—a woman—behind him. Dwight hit his brights and recognized Brenda's battered face even as his windshield was shattered and the sound of a gunshot echoed around them.

Dwight threw himself to the floorboard, drawing his pistol as he wedged himself beneath the steering column. "You can come out now, Deputy," a man's voice shouted. "Come out with your hands up and I promise I won't shoot you. But try anything and I'll kill your girlfriend here."

Dwight didn't answer. He glanced at the

radio, wondering if he could reach it and call for help. But a woman's scream, sharp and filled with pain, froze him. "Come out now!" the voice demanded. "Unless you want me to kill her now."

"I'm coming out!" Dwight answered, and raised his hands, though the rest of him remained shielded by the cruiser's door.

"Throw out your weapon."

Dwight tossed the gun onto the ground.

"Now come out with your hands up."

Everything within him resisted the idea of stepping out and exposing himself to the shooter, but the idea that Brenda could die if he hesitated propelled him to open the door and step into the open. A stocky man with a black knit ski mask pulled over his face held Brenda by one arm, a long-barreled pistol pressed to the side of her head. Brenda locked her eyes to Dwight's, determination shining through the fear. She trusted him to get them out of this, and that knowledge made him stronger.

"What do you want?" Dwight asked.

"I want the book," the man said.

"The Secret History of Rayford County?" Dwight wished he had urged Brenda to burn the book when she received the first threatening note.

"Yes. I want it."

"I don't have it."

The man drove the barrel of the gun into Brenda's cheek so that she cried out. "Don't lie to me!"

"The book is at the sheriff's department," Dwight said. "In the safe."

"Then we're going to go get it," the man said. He adjusted his grip on Brenda's arm. "But we don't need her to get it."

Instinct overwhelmed reason as Dwight realized what the man intended to do. With a roar, he launched himself at the other man, even as the pistol flashed in the darkness and the explosion of gunfire rang in the night stillness. Brenda's scream merged with his own cry of rage as he and the shooter grappled on the ground. Dwight clawed and kicked at the other man, who was shorter but heavier than him. And he knew how to fight.

He slammed his fist into the side of Dwight's head as Dwight grabbed hold of the pistol and tried to wrench it away. Dwight drove his elbow into the man's stomach, then thrust up his head, striking his assailant's chin and forcing his head back. The man roared in either pain or anger, and punched Dwight in the nose. Pain exploded behind his eyes and his vision went black, but he kept hold of the gun and struggled onto his knees, battling for equilibrium.

When the other man tried to kick him, Dwight scrambled out of the way, keeping hold of the gun and forcing the man's hand back at an awkward angle. The man cried out in pain, and Dwight shoved harder, putting all his weight behind the move. The man's fingers loosened, and Dwight seized the gun and trained it on the man.

But the other man shoved up to his feet and ran, the black of his clothing blending into the darkness. Dwight fired, but the shot went wide. Seconds later, the man was in the big SUV. Dwight steadied the gun with both hands and fired again, but only succeeded in taking out one taillight as the vehicle sped away.

Dazed and vaguely aware of blood streaming down his face, Dwight clutched the gun and tried to steady his breathing and think past the pain. A low moan cleared some of the fog engulfing him. "Brenda!" He looked around and heard the moan again, to his right. He unhooked his MagLite from his belt and played the beam along the shoulder of the road until he saw her. She lay back in the gravel and leaf litter, blood bathing her torso, her face ghostly white, her eyes closed.

"Brenda!" He shouted her name, but she

didn't stir. He shoved to his feet and ran to her, dropping to his knees beside her. "Brenda!" He took her hand, staring at the blood covering the front of her shirt.

She moaned again, and her eyes fluttered open. "Dwight." She struggled, as if trying to sit.

"Don't move." He put one hand on her shoulder to keep her from rising. "Where are you hurt?"

"My shoulder."

He trained the light on her left shoulder and surveyed the round hole that was seeping blood. The blood loss was a concern, but at least she hadn't been shot in the chest or stomach or head. "Lie still," he said. "I'm going to call for help and get the first aid kit from my cruiser."

"All right."

He ran to the cruiser, ignoring the pain from his nose, which was probably broken. Once there, he grabbed the radio, identified himself, asked for an ambulance for a gunshot victim and gave his location. "The shooter is a man about five ten, a hundred and eighty pounds, driving a black Land Rover, license Alfa, Foxtrot, Sierra, two, two, eight."

He retrieved the first aid kit and returned to Brenda. "I'm going to put some gauze on this wound and apply pressure to try to stop the bleeding," he said. "It might hurt, and I'm sorry about that."

"It's okay." She blinked at him, clearly dazed. "What happened to your face?"

He reached up and touched his nose, and winced as a fresh jolt of pain made him catch his breath. "I think the guy who shot you broke it."

"He ran me off the road," she said. "My car is down by the creek somewhere. My head hurts." She closed her eyes.

Did she have a concussion, too? Other injuries he didn't know about? "Talk to me," he said. "Try to stay awake. Do you know the guy? Did you recognize him from anywhere?"

"No. He wore a mask. Why did he shoot me?"

"I don't know." He made a thick pad from the gauze and pressed down hard on the wound. Brenda cried out and tried to roll away, but he held her firm. "We need to stop the bleeding," he said. "The ambulance will be here soon." Or he hoped it would be. If the ambulance crew were out on another call, it could take a while before they reached them. Meanwhile, he would do everything he could to help. "Do you think the man was Robert Brownley?" he asked.

She furrowed her brown. "Robert Browning? The poet?"

"Robert Brownley. The man who came to see you at the museum and wanted to bid on the book."

"I... I don't know." She looked at him, eyes full of questions behind the pain. "Why do you think that?"

"I recognized the SUV he was driving." In which case, Robert Brownley probably wasn't the man's real name, but Dwight had alerted his fellow law enforcement officers about the license plate of the Land Rover and the fact that it only had one taillight. He hoped someone would stop Brownley before he had time to ditch the vehicle and switch to another.

"I don't know," Brenda said. "I can't think very clearly right now."

"Don't worry about it now. Do you hurt anywhere else—besides your head and your shoulder?"

Before she could answer the question, headlight beams illuminated them, and tires crunched on gravel as a red Jeep Wagoneer pulled in in front of Dwight's cruiser. Still pressing down on the gauze pad, Dwight squinted over his shoulder at the vehicle and the man who climbed out of the driver's seat.

"What happened?" Eddie Carstairs asked, hurrying toward them.

"Brenda's been shot," Dwight said. "An ambulance is on its way. Maybe you can walk down the road a little ways and watch for it and flag it down."

"Sure." Eddie took a few steps closer. "Is she okay?"

"I'm going to be fine," Brenda said before Dwight could answer. The strength in her voice encouraged him. He reached out to stroke the side of her face.

"Yes, you're going to be fine," he said. "I think the bleeding has almost stopped."

"What happened?" Eddie asked again.

"Some guy ran her off the road and shot her," Dwight said. "He wanted that book—the one about the World War II laboratories. I got his plate number and every cop in the state will be looking for him soon."

"Looks like he almost got the better of

you," Eddie said, leaning down to peer at Dwight's face.

"Eddie, what are you doing here?" Brenda asked. "You're supposed to be at the museum."

"I came to find you. You and Dwight." He reached behind him and drew his gun. "I need you to take me to the book."

Chapter Sixteen

Dwight reached for his weapon, but Eddie lashed out, kicking him viciously. Brenda's scream echoed around them as Dwight fell back. When he sat up, Eddie had the gun trained on Brenda. "You need to cooperate with me or I'll shoot her." His voice shook a little, but his hand remained steady. "Don't think I won't do it."

"Eddie, why?" Brenda asked.

"Nothing personal against you," Eddie said. "But I'm sworn to do my duty." He motioned to Dwight. "Stand up. We need to get going."

Dwight stood, and Brenda struggled to prop

herself up on one elbow. "What do you mean, your duty?" she asked.

"I don't have time to explain now." He took Dwight's elbow. "We have to go."

Where is that ambulance? Dwight thought. "I'm not leaving Brenda," he said.

"Of course not," Eddie said. "Do you think I'm stupid enough to leave her to tell the paramedics where we are and what we're doing? She's coming with us."

"She's injured," Dwight protested. "She needs medical care."

"Then I'll just have to finish her off." Eddie shifted the gun toward her.

"No!" Brenda struggled to sit, one hand keeping the gauze pad in place over her wound. "I'll go with you. You just have to help me up." This last she directed at Dwight. He wanted to argue that she should lie still, but he didn't trust Eddie not to carry out his threat to kill her. The security guard looked desperate and a little unhinged.

"It's going to be all right," Dwight whispered in Brenda's ear as he helped her to stand. "Just hang in there." Eddie thought they were at his mercy, but at the first opportunity, Dwight would prove he was wrong.

BRENDA FOUGHT WAVES of nausea and dizziness as Dwight half carried her to Eddie's Jeep. Her shoulder throbbed with pain, and she took shallow breaths, trying to avoid moving it. But that didn't help much, as every step over the rough ground jarred the wound. Dwight pressed the gauze tightly against her, adding to the agony, though she knew it was necessary to keep her from bleeding to death. She fought back panic. She wasn't going to die. Not over some stupid book.

Not when she had finally found Dwight.

Eddie stood beside them while Dwight helped her climb into the Jeep. She loathed the idea of sitting next to Eddie, but he wasn't giving her any choice. When Dwight had buckled her seat belt, Eddie prodded him with the gun. "Now let's take care of your cruiser."

"What about my cruiser?" Dwight asked.

"You don't think I'm stupid enough to let you leave it here, where anyone coming along might see it and call in a report about an abandoned cop vehicle?" He jabbed Dwight in the shoulder with the gun. "Come on."

Dwight looked at Brenda. Maybe if she'd been in better shape, she could have used this opportunity to run for help, but it was taking every ounce of strength she could muster to remain upright in the truck. "I'll be right back," Dwight said.

She nodded.

As soon as he had left her, she closed her eyes, but opened them again as that seemed to make the dizziness worse. She studied the contents of Eddie's Jeep—fast-food wrappers and discarded cups stained with coffee littered the floormats, while gas receipts, maps and other papers almost obscured the dashboard.

She saw nothing in the debris that gave her a clue as to why he was doing this. Were he and the man who had shot her working together— or were they rivals, both wanting *The Secret History of Rayford County, Colorado* for some reason?

Maybe all this had something to do with money, she thought. Eddie struck her as a man who was very motivated by money. He was always talking about how hard up he was since he had been let go from the sheriff's department—even though as a reserve officer, he had worked only part time and made very little. But it was probably easier to blame Travis for his woes than admit that his own actions had led to his downfall.

An engine raced, startling her. She raised her eyes to the rearview mirror and gasped as Dwight's SUV rolled toward the drop-off on the opposite side of the road. The front wheels left the pavement and the vehicle lurched forward, then tumbled over the edge, the sound of it hitting and bouncing off the rocks echoing in the still night air.

The two men returned to the Jeep. Dwight's hands were cuffed behind his back—Brenda assumed with his own handcuffs. Eddie waited until he had slid into the passenger seat beside Brenda, then he shut the door and walked around to the driver's side. "What are we going to do?" Brenda whispered.

"Wait for an opportunity," Dwight said.

Eddie slammed the door behind him and put the Jeep into gear. He held the gun in his right hand, his left on the steering wheel. "Just remember, Dwight. If you try anything, I'll shoot Brenda. I know you don't want that."

Dwight said nothing, though Brenda felt his tension, the muscles of his forearm taut beside her. "Where are we going?" she asked as Eddie turned the truck back toward town.

"We're going to get that book out of the safe."

"Why do you want the book?" she asked.

But he didn't answer as the flashing lights of

an ambulance approached, the siren wailing. Eddie slowed and edged to the shoulder, turning his face away as the ambulance passed, bathing the interior of the Jeep in red light. When it was past, Eddie pulled onto the highway again.

Maybe someone will be at the sheriff's department when we arrive, Brenda thought. But as soon as they pulled into the dark, empty lot, she knew that was a false hope. The force was so small they often had only one or two officers on duty overnight, and they spent most of their time in the field, patrolling. No one else was out at this late hour, either, the streets empty of cars or pedestrians. A quarter moon rose over Dakota Ridge, stars like sequins on a cocktail dress shining around it. Under other circumstances, she would have admired the view. A new pain shot through her as she wondered if this would be the last night she ever saw these stars.

Eddie drove around the back of the sheriff's department and parked in the shadow of the building. Security lights bathed the area around the back door in a silvery-white glow, but inside Eddie's truck was pitch-black. "Where are your keys?" he asked Dwight.

"My front pocket."

Eddie nudged Brenda with the gun. "Get them," he ordered.

She looked to Dwight. He nodded and lifted his hip to make it easier for her to reach into his pocket and retrieve the keys. She handed them to Eddie. "All right," he said. "We're going to all go in, and you're going to get the book out of the safe. And remember—you try anything and Brenda is dead."

The words sent a chill through her, but she fought back the fear. She had to stay calm and alert for any chance to help get them out of this. They climbed out of the Jeep. She had to hold on to Dwight's shoulder to stand, she felt so shaky and weak. "Come on," Eddie said, one leg bouncing with agitation. "We don't have all night."

They made their way toward the door. Before they reached it, Eddie shot out the security camera focused over it. Brenda stifled a scream as the report of the gun rang in her ears. A second shot took out the light. Maybe someone would hear the shots and come to investigate, she thought. If only they would come in time.

The security keypad beside the door glowed with a red light. "What's your code?" Eddie asked.

Dwight said nothing.

"Give me the code." Eddie grabbed Brenda's arm—the wounded one—and jerked her toward him. Pain blinded her and she screamed, her knees giving way.

"One six three four," Dwight said. He bent over Brenda. "Are you all right?"

It was a moment before she could speak. She struggled to control her breathing and managed to nod, then, realizing he might not be able to see her in the dark, said, "Yes."

"Get up," Eddie said, then he turned and punched in the code.

Hands bound behind his back, Dwight couldn't help her, but he braced himself so that she could pull herself up against him. She leaned on him for a moment, still breathing hard, while Eddie opened the door. Then he motioned them inside.

He led the way down a flight of stairs to a small room at the back of the building, and used a second key to unlock it. When he flipped on the light, Brenda saw shelves full of guns and ammunition. Eddie moved aside a cardboard box labeled "SWAT" to reveal a small safe. "What's the combination?" he asked.

"It's in the sheriff's office," Dwight said.

Eddie looked at Brenda.

"I'm telling the truth!" Dwight said. "Why would I have the combination to the safe?"

"You put the book in the safe after you took it from the museum tonight, didn't you?" Eddie asked.

"It was open. The book was the only thing in the safe, so when we removed the book, we left it open. All I did when I put it back in there was close the door."

"Then come on." They trooped back down the hall and up the stairs to Travis's office. The door was closed, but not locked. "Where does he keep the combination?" Eddie asked.

"There's a shelf that pulls out on the right-hand side," Dwight said.

Eddie found the shelf and pulled it out. A piece of paper was taped to it. From her position by the door, Brenda could see what looked like a list of phone numbers, but apparently, the combination to the safe was there, too.

"I really need to sit down," she said, and sank into the chair across from Travis's desk.

Eddie scowled at her. "Get up."

"I can't," she said, her voice so weak she

could hardly hear it. She closed her eyes. She didn't really care what happened to her now. She was beginning to think she was going to die, anyway.

"Leave her alone," Dwight said. "You've got your combination. Go get the book."

Eddie glared at them, as if about to argue, then jerked his head up. "Is that a siren?" he asked.

Brenda heard nothing, but Dwight said, "Someone must have heard those shots you fired."

Eddie sprinted out of the office and down the hall. Dwight bent over Brenda. "Hang on just a little longer," he said.

She opened her eyes and focused on his hands, the wrists bound with the silver cuffs. "Do you think someone is really coming?" she asked.

"I didn't hear anything," he said. "I think Eddie might be cracking up, but we'll take advantage of that. Can you get the key out of my pocket and unlock these cuffs?" He turned so that his other side faced her.

Energized by the prospect of freeing him, she found the key. He turned his back and held out his hands to her. She fumbled with the lock at first, but after a moment, he was free.

He rubbed his wrists, then put his hand on her uninjured shoulder. "Come with me to my office and hide there," he said.

He helped her up and together they made their way as quietly as possible across the hall to the office Dwight shared with Gage. She sat in his chair while he slid open the bottom drawer of the desk and took out a pistol. He checked to make sure it was loaded, then bent and kissed her cheek. "Wait here," he said, then slipped quietly out of the room.

Brenda clutched her wounded shoulder and rested her head on the desk. She prayed this nightmare would be over soon—and that Dwight would come out the winner. Eddie definitely seemed unbalanced, but that just made him more dangerous.

DWIGHT MOVED AS quickly and as soundlessly as possible toward the door of the armory. Eddie probably had the safe open by now. What would he do when he had the book? Would he simply leave? The supposed siren had seemingly spurred him to grab the book and make his escape, but maybe he would come back to finish off the witnesses to his crime.

Dwight stopped outside the door to the room. Eddie had turned on the overhead light and he stood beside the safe, the book in his hand. He was tearing pages from the book, a few at a time, and dropping them into a metal trash can. As Dwight stared, he took a cigarette lighter from his pocket and touched the flame to the edge of one of the pages. The paper flared, and Eddie dropped it into the trash can with the rest.

Dwight braced himself and aimed the gun. "Eddie Carstairs, you're under arrest," he said.

Eddie turned, openmouthed, and started to raise his gun. Dwight fired, and Eddie lurched away, so that the bullet caught him in the shoulder—almost exactly the spot where Brenda had been shot.

Eddie dropped the gun and sank to his knees beside the trash can, the contents of which were burning brightly, filling the small room with smoke. Dwight scowled at the blaze, then kicked Eddie's gun out of the way. He grabbed him by the arm and hauled him up. "Get up!" he ordered. "Or do you want to give me an excuse to shoot you again?"

Eddie said nothing, but stood and let Dwight push him down the hall to the holding cell. He cuffed him by one hand to the metal grating of the cell and locked the door behind him. About that time the smoke alarm started blaring. Dwight grabbed a fire extinguisher and ran to douse the trash can in the armory, then pulled out his phone and called for an ambulance as he jogged down the hall to Brenda.

He stopped in the doorway of his office. She had her head down on the desk, and she was so still he went ice cold. "Brenda?" he asked.

No reaction. Heart in his throat, he crossed the room and knelt beside her. When he laid his hand on her back, she stirred and raised her head. "What happened?" she asked.

"It's over," Dwight said. "Eddie's locked in a cell." He didn't tell her that he had shot him. She'd find that out soon enough. "Are you okay?"

She tried to smile, though succeeded only in lifting the corners of her mouth a scant half inch. "I've been better."

"Hang on," he said. "The ambulance is on its way."

"I'm not going anywhere." She rested her cheek against his hand and closed her eyes. "Not when I've finally found you."

He wanted to ask her what she meant by that,

but had no time, as someone was pounding on the door, demanding to be let in. He stood and went to answer it, light-headed and a little unsteady on his feet, but how much of that was the adrenaline that had flooded him earlier draining away and how much was sheer love for this woman who had endured so much, he couldn't say.

Chapter Seventeen

Dwight sipped the tepid hospital coffee and tried to will away the fog of sleeplessness that dulled his senses. The early-morning hours had passed in a blur of dealing with the ambulance and the sheriff, who arrived as the paramedics were wheeling Brenda out of the sheriff's department. A second ambulance arrived a few minutes later to transport Eddie to the hospital. Travis agreed to go with Eddie, while Dwight followed Brenda.

They had agreed to team up this morning to question Eddie, as soon as doctors gave the go-ahead for them to do so. Dwight stared into the dregs of the coffee and decided he had had enough. He tossed it in the trash can and turned toward the door of the surgery floor waiting room just as Travis walked in. Despite having been awake as many hours as Dwight, Travis managed to look as sharp as ever. Dwight narrowed his eyes at his boss. "How is it you look ready to lead a parade and I feel like death warmed over?" he asked.

"I went home and showered and shaved," Travis said. "Gage is keeping an eye on Eddie, though I don't think he's in any shape to go anywhere."

"The bullet shattered his collarbone." Dwight grimaced. "If he hadn't jerked away, it would have been a heart shot."

Travis put a hand on Dwight's shoulder. "If you hadn't shot him, he would have killed you. Say what you will about the job Eddie did as a reserve officer, but he was always one of the top qualifiers at the range."

"I'd forgotten about that." Not that it would

have made any difference in how he had reacted last night—his life had been in danger
and his training had kicked in to protect him.

"His doctor says we can have a few minutes
with him," Travis said. "He's on pain medica-
tion, but lucid."

"Let's hope the meds loosen his tongue
enough for him to tell us what's going on,"
Dwight said. Though even then, a good lawyer might argue that Eddie had revealed information under the influence of narcotics. They
had enough other evidence against Eddie that
it was a chance Travis felt they could take.

"How is Brenda?" Travis asked.

"She's going to be fine." Saying the words
out loud made him feel a little lighter. "The
surgeon was able to remove the bullet, and he
said there's no permanent damage. I looked
in on her a little while ago, but she was still
sleeping."

"I'm glad to hear it," Travis said. "Are you
ready to talk to Eddie?"

"I am." He had a lot of things he would like to say to the man who had harassed and almost killed Brenda, but most of them he would have to keep to himself. Knowing Eddie was going to prison for a very long time to pay for what he had done would have to be enough.

Eddie's room was at the opposite end of the corridor from Brenda's. Since he was technically in the custody of the Rayford County Sheriff's Department, he rated a private room, and a guard on duty outside his door 24-7. Gage rose from a chair he'd placed against the wall opposite that door as Travis and Dwight approached.

"He's awake," Gage said after the three men exchanged greetings. "I looked in on him a few minutes ago and he wanted to tell me about how none of this was his fault, but I told him to save it for you two."

"Not his fault?" Dwight shook his head. "This should be interesting."

Gage checked his phone. "I need to get going if I'm going to make the auction."

"The auction?" Dwight asked. With everything that had happened in the last few hours, he had forgotten all about the museum's auction.

"Lacy and Paige decided that they needed to go ahead with it, since some of the bidders are here from out of town," Travis said. "They wanted to do it for Brenda."

"I'm sure she'll appreciate it," Dwight said. "Of course, the most valuable item is gone. All that's left of *The Secret History of Rayford Country, Colorado* is a bucket of wet ashes."

"They still want to get what they can," Gage said. "I'm going to run security, along with one of the reserve officers."

"You'd better go, then," Travis said. "We can handle things on this end." He pushed open the door to Eddie's room.

A muted television, and a bank of monitors provided the only illumination in the room.

Eddie lay on his back in the bed, the head elevated forty-five degrees, a mass of white bandages around his left shoulder. His right hand was cuffed to the railing of the bed, an IV tube trailing from it. He turned his head toward them, his skin pale against a day's growth of dark beard and the cuts and bruises from his struggles with Dwight. "Hello, Sheriff," he said, his voice surprisingly clear.

"Hello, Eddie." Travis stopped beside the bed. "We need to ask you some questions about what happened yesterday."

"I know. And I can explain everything. I—"

Travis held up one hand. "Before you say anything, I need to tell you that you have the right to remain silent. Anything you say could be held against you in a court of law. You have the right to have an attorney present. If you cannot afford an attorney, one will be appointed by the courts."

"I know my rights," Eddie said. "I read them

off to other people enough. I don't need a lawyer for what I have to say to you."

Dwight moved in on the other side of the
bed. Eddie turned his head to look at him.
"How is Brenda doing?" he asked.

"Why are you even asking?" Dwight said,
unable to hold in his anger.

"If she'd just cooperated like I asked her to,
none of this would have happened," he said,
his voice a plaintive whine.

"Were you the one who sent those threatening notes to Brenda?" Travis asked.

"I didn't do it for myself," Eddie said. "It
was a matter of national security. All she had
to do was get rid of that book."

Travis's and Dwight's eyes met across the
bed. *National security?* "Why was that book
so important?" Travis asked.

"The man who hired me told me I had to
make sure it was destroyed so that it didn't
fall into the wrong hands."

"Who was this man?" Travis asked.

"I don't know his real name," Dwight said. "He told me to call him B."

"Bee?" Dwight asked.

"The letter B. He called me E. They were, like, code names. He worked for a top-secret government agency."

"Did he show you credentials?" Travis asked.

"Of course he did." Eddie looked indignant. "I'm not stupid."

"And his credentials said his name was B?" Dwight asked.

"Yes." Eddie glared at them.

"What branch of the government was he from?" Travis asked.

Eddie frowned. "Something top secret. I mean, his credentials said Department of Homeland Security, but the more we talked, the more I got the impression that he was really CIA or something like that."

"What did he promise you in exchange for your help?" Travis asked.

"He told me he could get me a job with the Secret Service."

"Is that all?" Travis asked.

"He paid me a lot of money. Ten thousand dollars. Don't look at me that way! Since you fired me from the sheriff's department, my bills have been piling up. I needed that money."

Travis leaned over the bed railing. "Eddie, why would the Feds ask you to threaten Brenda Stenson?"

"I wasn't threatening her. I was just, you know, intimidating her so that she'd get rid of that book. B said it was a security risk and we couldn't let it fall into the wrong hands."

"Did he say why?" Travis asked.

"No."

"Did you ask?" Dwight asked.

Eddie looked even more sullen. "No."

"Did you burn down Brenda's house?" Dwight asked.

Eddie shifted in the bed. "I think I need to speak to my lawyer."

"You're in this so deep no lawyer is going to be able to get you out," Dwight said. "Your only chance is to help us get to the truth."

"B was putting a lot of pressure on me. He said I was failing my country. I figured if I destroyed her house, I'd destroy the book and the problem would be solved. I figured she had insurance, and I knew she wasn't home. I mean, I'd never hurt her, even if she does treat me like something she scraped off the bottom of her shoe."

"Where did you get that crime scene photo of Andy Stenson?" Dwight asked.

Eddie flushed and looked away. "I don't see why that matters."

"Did you take it from the case file when you were with the department?" Travis asked.

"You'll never prove it," Eddie said.

"What do you know about Henry Hake's death?" Travis asked.

"Nothing! I didn't have anything to do with that. All I did was try to get Brenda to get rid of that book, like B asked. You find him and he'll tell you."

"How do we get in touch with him?" Travis asked.

"I don't know. He always got in touch with me. But he must be staying nearby. Maybe you could just call the Department of Homeland Security and ask."

"We will," Travis said. Though Dwight had his doubts they would find out anything.

"What was in the book that was so important?" Travis asked. "Did he give you any indication?"

"I already told you, I don't know. He said I didn't need to know."

No one would know now, Dwight thought, since the book had been destroyed.

"I know you think what I did was wrong," Eddie said. "But I didn't have a choice. B threatened to kill me if I didn't get the job done—the sleeping-pill-laced pizza was supposed to prove how easily he could get to me."

"Was B the man you were meeting with at the restaurant that night Brenda and Lacy and the others saw you?" Dwight asked. "Did he slash the tires on Parker's car?"

"I don't know anything about that. And I'm not going to say anything else." He sagged back against the pillow, his face pale. "I'm exhausted and in pain. You can't badger me this way."

Travis looked at Dwight and jerked his head toward the door. Dwight followed him out. "Do you buy his story, about all this being his patriotic duty?" Dwight asked.

"I think the money and the promise of the Secret Service job and the idea of being a hero would appeal to him," Travis said. "I'll talk to Lacy and get her description of the man who was with Eddie that night at the restaurant."

"I remember Brenda saying they didn't get a good look at the man—his face was in shadow."

"We'll get what we can."

"I'm wondering if B was Robert Brownley," Dwight said. "If he's the one who gave Eddie the doctored pizza, we know he was at the museum that evening."

"Good thinking," Travis said. "Get Brownley's description from Brenda and we'll compare notes."

"I'm going down to check on her now," Dwight said. "If she's awake, I'll ask her."

BRENDA HAD BEEN awake for some time that morning. There was nothing like a near-death experience to make a person take stock of her life. She had made some bad decisions, and had had more than her share of bad breaks, but instead of focusing on the past, she needed to come up with a plan for the future.

A light tapping attracted her attention to the door. Dwight leaned in. "Feel like some company?" he asked.

"Definitely." She found the controls for the

bed and elevated the head so that she could get a better look at him.

"Why are you frowning at me?" he asked, coming to stand beside her.

"You look worn out," she said. Two black eyes from his broken nose and the dark shadow of beard along his jaw made him look dangerous—and utterly weary. "Have you been home at all since last night?"

"I'll go in a little bit. I wanted to make sure you were all right."

She reached up and took his hand. He squeezed it, and the tenderness in his touch made her feel a little choked up. She cleared her throat. If she started crying, he would think something was wrong. "I'm going to be fine," she said. "The surgeon said so. I can probably go home this afternoon."

"You'll come back to my place," he said.

She might have argued, but why bother? With him was where she wanted to be. "That sounds good. But it's going to be a while, so you should try to get a few hours' sleep. I can get Lacy to take me to you if you aren't back when the doctor signs the discharge papers."

"Lacy is going to be busy for a while," he said.

"Oh? What? Did she and Travis decide to elope or something?"

He smiled, a little more life coming into his eyes. "Nothing like that. But she and Paige are handling the auction at the museum."

"The auction?" She tried to sit up, and regretted it as pain shot through her bandaged shoulder. With a groan, she settled back against the pillows. "I've been lying here, trying to convince myself that it didn't matter that we had to cancel the auction. But they're going through with it?"

"With some of the bidders here from out of town, they figured they had better."

"That's so sweet of them. Though the most valuable item we had is gone now."

"You still had a lot of items left. You'll bring in a good chunk of change."

Not enough, she thought. But no sense dwelling on that. "How is Eddie?" she asked. "I know they rushed him into surgery before me."

"His recovery is going to take a little longer, but he'll live." Dwight certainly wasn't smiling now. "He admitted he sent you those threatening letters—and he burned down your house."

"But why?" She had scarcely said a dozen words to Eddie Carstairs in all the years they had both lived in Eagle Mountain.

"Apparently, someone posing as a federal agent offered him a lot of money to make sure the book was destroyed."

"What was so important about that book?" she asked. "I read through it more than once and I couldn't see anything significant there."

"I don't know. And Eddie says he doesn't know, either."

"Then why would he agree to do it—to harass me and commit arson—even threaten to kill the two of us? Surely he isn't that hard up and greedy."

"You know Eddie always wanted to be a hero. This man—who I don't for a minute believe was really with the government—convinced Eddie that he had to destroy the book to keep it out of enemy hands—that it was a matter of national security. When Eddie failed the first couple of tries, this mysterious agent delivered that doctored pizza—supposedly to prove how easily he could kill Eddie if he wanted to. That made him desperate to fulfill his 'mission.'"

Brenda tried to take this all in. "That's incredible. Do you think this mysterious secret agent is the one who ran me off the road and shot me?"

"Maybe."

"Did Eddie tell you how to find this supposed agent?" she asked.

"He says he doesn't know. The only name he has is B. But I'm wondering if it was Robert

Brownley—or rather, the man who came to you posing as Robert Brownley. I don't think that's his real name."

"He was very insistent on getting his hands on the book that night. And I'll admit he seemed rather menacing." She shivered, remembering being alone with the man.

"Do you think the man who attacked you and the man who posed as Robert Brownley were the same person?" Dwight asked.

"I don't know. It was dark and he wore that mask." She shook her head. "Maybe."

"I need you to give me your description of him again," Dwight said. "We're going to use every resource we can to find him."

She closed her eyes, trying to remember. "So much has happened since then," she said. "I don't know if I can give you enough information."

"Take your time. Describe him to me—what he looked like, as well as your impressions."

"He was in his forties, I think. Average

height and build. Dark hair. His eyes were light—gray, I think, and really intense. I guess my biggest impression of him was that he was the kind of man who was used to getting what he wanted. Powerful—but personality-wise, not so much physically. He was well-dressed. His suit looked expensive, not off-the-rack. And he drove that black Land Rover—not a cheap car." Her eyes met Dwight's. "He looked like what he said he was—a rich business-man."

"I may ask you to look at some photographs later and see if you recognize him."

"I'll do whatever I can to help."

"We may be too late," Dwight said. "My guess is that now that he got what he wanted and the book is gone, he'll leave the county, maybe even the country."

"Give Travis my description and then prom-ise me you'll go home and get some sleep," she said. "You're not going to be good to anyone if you fall asleep at the wheel of your cruiser."

"I could get used to you nagging me that way." He leaned over and kissed her on the lips. When he started to pull away, she grabbed his collar and prolonged the embrace. When at last she released him, he looked decidedly less weary. Later, they would talk, and she would tell him some things she had decided.

In the meantime, she liked giving him something to think about.

Chapter Eighteen

Dwight gave Travis Brenda's description of Brownley, then did as he had promised and went home, where he slept for four hours before a phone call awakened him. Groggily, he groped for the cell phone and answered it.

"You need to get back to the hospital," Travis said. "The judge is on her way over to conduct the arraignment for Eddie."

Dwight checked the clock at his bedside—it was almost one in the afternoon. "That was quick."

"Frank Rizzo is Eddie's attorney. He pulled some strings to rush the arraignment."

"Frank Rizzo? How did Eddie afford him?" Rizzo had represented a number of high-profile, very wealthy defendants.

"Eddie was as surprised to see Rizzo as I was," Travis said. "He said obviously the government had come through to support him. He's practically giddy, and I don't think it's all from the painkillers his doctor prescribed. He's convinced he's going to be exonerated as a national hero."

"I'm going to shower and change, and I'll be right over," Dwight said.

By the time Dwight arrived at the hospital, the lot was crowded with news vans and broadcast trucks from every major television and radio network. Dwight's uniform attracted their attention, and he found himself pushing through a crowd of reporters with microphones who demanded to know what his role was in the case. He ignored them and made his way inside.

Fortunately, the hospital's corridors were

closed to reporters. Travis met Dwight outside Eddie's room. "Did Rizzo alert the media?" Dwight asked.

"Probably," Travis said. "That's his style."

The man himself stepped out of Eddie's room and closed the door behind him. Clean-shaven and bald, dressed in a gray wool suit and wearing old-school horn-rimmed glasses, Frank Rizzo was well-known to television viewers and readers of the most popular gossip mags. From professional athletes to B-list celebrities to corporate moguls, his client list was a who's who of misbehaving millionaires. His eyes narrowed when he saw Dwight. "Deputy Prentice?" he asked.

Dwight nodded.

"You're the man who shot my client," Rizzo said.

"Your client was shooting at me at the time."

"So you say. My client has a different story."

Dwight kept quiet. Rizzo liked to goad his opponents into saying things he could use against them in court. Dwight wouldn't play his game.

"The judge is here," Travis said. The three men turned to see an older woman with silver-blond hair, dressed in a red business suit, striding down the hallway, followed by a young man who was carrying a court stenographer's machine and a second man who was probably the clerk of the court. Several feet behind them came a very tall man in a blue suit—District Attorney Scott Percy.

The woman stopped in front of them. "Judge Miranda Geisel." She shook hands with each of them in turn. "Let's get this proceeding started."

Travis entered the room first, followed by the judge and her attendants, the DA and Frank Rizzo, with Dwight bringing up the rear. He stationed himself by the door, while the others crowded around the bed, jostling for position in the small space.

The man who had harassed Brenda, destroyed her home and her car, and threatened to kill her, managed to look frail and vulnerable in the hospital bed, his shoulder bandaged and his unshaven face white with pain.

Judge Geisel looked around and, apparently satisfied that all was as it should be, nodded. "Let's begin, gentlemen."

The clerk read off the date, time and nature of the proceedings for the record, then listed the charges against Eddie. Though Dwight was aware of all of them, read together they formed an impressive list—everything from harassment to arson to theft to attempted murder. It would be a very long time before Eddie was a free man again.

"How does your client plead?" Judge Geisel asked.

"Not guilty, Your Honor," said Rizzo.

No surprise there, despite the fact that Eddie had been caught red-handed in the commission of the most serious charge, and had admitted to most of the others. Rizzo would no doubt be contesting those previous confessions. Dwight was almost looking forward to hearing the defense's case, especially if Rizzo could produce the mysterious B.

"I request that my client be released on his own recognizance," Rizzo said.

"The nature of these crimes are such that we request Mr. Carstairs be held without bail," Percy countered.

Eddie watched this exchange, wide-eyed, his gaze shifting from one side of the bed to the other.

"These are very serious charges," the judge said.

"Your Honor, my client has absolutely no record of previous violence," Rizzo said. "He isn't a flight risk. The man is seriously injured and will be recovering for some time."

"My understanding is that Mr. Carstairs could be released from the hospital as early as this afternoon," the judge said.

"If you will authorize his release, I will be

personally transporting him to a rehab facility," Rizzo said. "You don't have to worry about him getting into trouble there."

"Your Honor, Mr. Carstairs tried to kill a woman and a police officer," Percy said. "He has been relentless in his pursuit of Mrs. Stenson and remains a threat to her still."

"As Mr. Rizzo has pointed out, Mr. Carstairs's injuries are such that he can't drive a car or go much of anywhere," the judge said. "I think that mitigates the threat. And I am cognizant of the burden on the county if he must remain in protective custody while undergoing rehabilitation and continued medical treatment." She turned to Rizzo. "I'm setting bail at $500,000."

"Your Honor, Mr. Carstairs is unemployed," Rizzo said. "He can't possibly afford such a sum."

"Yet he can somehow afford your fees," the judge said. "Or are you doing pro bono work these days, Mr. Rizzo?"

Rizzo compressed his lips into a thin line and said nothing.

"Bail is set at $500,000," she repeated. "This arraignment is adjourned."

No one said anything while the court reporter packed up his recording equipment. Travis and Dwight left Rizzo to confer with his client and followed the court personnel and the DA into the hall. Percy waited until the judge and her staff had left before he spoke. "No surprise on the bail," he said. "And she's right—in his condition, I don't think he's a flight risk."

"I'm not so sure about that," Dwight said. "He's got someone behind the scenes pulling strings."

"I figured someone else was paying Rizzo's fees," Percy said. "Any idea who?"

"We're still digging," Travis said.

"All that stuff in the report you sent me about secret government agents—do you believe any of that?" Percy asked.

"No," Travis said.

The door opened and Rizzo stepped out. "I'm going to make arrangements for Eddie's release," he said. "I'll see you gentlemen in court."

They watched him walk down the hall and enter the elevator. "Want to bet he stops off downstairs to talk to the media?" Percy asked.

"No bets," Travis said.

"This is going to be an interesting one," Percy said.

They said goodbye and he left them. "I'll take over guarding Eddie," Dwight said. "I know you have things to do."

"I think it's best if you limit your contact with him," Travis said. "Just in case Rizzo follows through with any countersuit. Besides, I know you want to be with Brenda."

"She's supposed to be discharged this afternoon," Dwight said. "I'd like to take her home."

"Go." Travis clamped him on the back. "I'll take care of things here."

Dwight found Brenda in a wheelchair beside her bed, wearing a pink hospital gown and fuzzy pink socks. She could have been wrapped up in old sacking for all Dwight cared. The fact that she was upright and smiling made her the most beautiful person he would ever see.

"You look much better," she said, tilting her cheek up for him to kiss. "Did you get some sleep?"

"A little." He rubbed his smooth chin. "A shower and a shave helped, too."

"I just talked to Lacy. She said the auction made over $20,000. A lot more than I expected, since we no longer had the book."

"That will keep you going another few months at least," Dwight said. "It will give you more time to find a new benefactor."

"Professor Gibson may have come through for us there. He said he was so impressed with the museum, he's recommended us to the Falmont Foundation."

Dwight sat on the end of the bed, so that they were more or less at eye level. "What is the Falmont Foundation?" he asked.

"You know the Falmont family—Falmont semiconductors?"

He shook his head. "Never heard of them."

"It doesn't matter. They have a charitable trust that gives money to worthy causes. Apparently, Julius Falmont was a great history buff. And Professor Gibson used to be on the board of the trust. He's recommended us for underwriting. This could be exactly what we've been hoping for." Her eyes shone, and Dwight couldn't remember when she had looked so happy.

"That's great," he said. "It's good to know all the hard work you've put into the museum is getting the recognition it deserves."

"I don't know about that—I'm just glad we

don't have to close the doors and I don't have to start looking for another job."

He stood. "Are you ready to go home?"

"I'm ready, but we're still waiting on the doctor to sign the paperwork. A nurse is trying to locate him now."

Dwight sat back down. "We just had Eddie's arraignment," he said.

"Already?" she asked.

"The judge came here. It's not unusual when someone being charged with a crime is hospitalized. He's being released on bail. Somehow, he has Frank Rizzo as his attorney."

"He's being released?" Much of the elation went out of her face.

"To a rehab center." He took her hand. "He's not in any shape to harm you anymore—and I'll be keeping an eye out for you."

She nodded. "I guess I'm just surprised he would be released."

"He doesn't have a criminal history, and he's not considered a threat at the moment,"

Dwight said. "Plus, I'm sure having Rizzo as an attorney helped. He has a reputation for making life miserable for judges who don't do what he wants. He has lots of friends in the media."

"How did Eddie afford someone like Frank Rizzo?" she asked.

"I don't know, but that's one thing we'll try to find out." He squeezed her hand. "I don't want you to worry. I'm going to keep you safe—even though I know you don't like relying on others."

Her eyes met his, a new softness in her face. "I've been doing a lot of thinking, and I've come to some decisions," she said.

He tensed. Was this when she told him "thanks, but no thanks" to any prospect of a relationship? "I don't know that now is the best time to be making decisions," he said.

"Hush, and let me talk." She tempered the words with a smile. "I realized as I was lying in that bed, reviewing everything that has happened to me over the last couple of years, that I've been going about things the wrong way. I've been reacting to whatever happened by becoming defensive. Andy was killed and I kept to myself, upset and ashamed and really, not coping very well. Then I found out he was blackmailing people in town and using the money to renovate our house and I reacted again, this time by deciding not to trust other people—not to trust other men. Not to trust you."

He waited, afraid of saying the wrong thing if he interrupted her.

"But just reacting to what other people did was the wrong approach, I think. Instead, I needed to step back and focus on what *I* want to happen. Where *I* want to go in life." She took a deep breath and let it out slowly. "It's time to follow my feelings instead of my fears. I love you, Dwight, and I think you love me."

"I do love you," he said. "I have for years."

She smiled again, and he felt like shouting

for joy. But all he did was remain very still, holding her hand and waiting to hear what she had to say next. "Life is too short for us to be apart anymore," she said.

"Yes." Then he did what he had wanted to do for weeks now—maybe even years. He dropped to his knees in front of the wheelchair. "Brenda Stenson, will you marry me?" he asked.

"Yes," she whispered, tears glinting in her eyes.

He leaned forward and kissed her, a long, passionate kiss to seal their pledge. And that was how the doctor found them when he and a nurse walked in.

"Well, it looks like you're feeling much better," he said as Brenda and Dwight moved apart and Dwight stood. The doctor scribbled his signature on the papers on a clipboard the nurse handed him. "Follow the instructions the nurse will give you and I'll see you in my office next week."

The doctor left and the nurse took charge of the wheelchair. Dwight gathered up Brenda's things and followed her into the hallway. They stopped short at the turn to the elevator when they saw Eddie, also in a wheelchair, with Frank Rizzo at his side. "Stop," Brenda ordered.

They stopped and waited for Eddie and his attorney to pass. Neither man looked their way. When the elevator doors closed behind them, Brenda sagged against the chair. "Eddie looked bad," she said. "I'm still not happy about him getting bail, but he really doesn't look like a threat." She looked up at the nurse. "Okay, we can go now."

They arrived downstairs to a scene of chaos. People filled the front lobby, many of them members of the press with cameras and microphones. "I should have thought of this," Dwight said. "We need to go out the back entrance."

But they had already been spotted. A trio

of reporters and cameramen surged toward them, shouting questions. Brenda covered her face. "No comment," Dwight shouted. He took control of the wheelchair and pushed toward the doors.

But their progress was blocked again by Frank Rizzo, who stood in the portico, holding forth to an audience of media and bystanders. More cameras flashed as he proclaimed his client's innocence. Eddie slumped in his wheelchair beside Rizzo, the picture of the aggrieved victim of injustice.

Dwight was searching for the best escape route when Rizzo concluded his comments, just as a black sedan pulled into the portico. Rizzo wheeled his client toward the waiting car, then someone screamed. At almost the same moment, the *pock!* of a silenced weapon sounded, and Eddie sagged further down in his chair.

"Get her inside!" Dwight shoved the wheelchair toward a man in scrubs, then sprinted toward Eddie. A bloom of red spread across Eddie's chest. Around them, people screamed, some dropping to the ground, others fleeing either back into the building or across the parking lot.

Another man, also wearing scrubs, reached Eddie at the same time as Dwight and felt for a pulse. He shook his head. "He's gone," he said.

Dwight looked around. Frank Rizzo and the black sedan were both gone also, though Dwight was sure the shots had come from farther away—possibly the parking garage across from the main hospital building.

Two uniformed police officers ran up to him. "Did anyone see the shooter?" the older of the two, a muscular black man, asked.

"No. But I think he might have been firing from the parking garage," Dwight said.

The officer studied the parking structure. "Long shot," he said.

"Not too long for a professional," Dwight said. He had no doubt Eddie's murder had been carefully orchestrated. Someone—B?—didn't want him to tell whatever he knew.

DWIGHT SPENT THE rest of the day running down leads that went nowhere. He and local police searched the parking garage and the area around the hospital and came up with nothing—no video, no eyewitnesses, no bullet casings, no foot impressions—nothing. One more indication that whoever had killed Eddie was a professional.

Lacy showed up with Travis and offered to drive Brenda to Dwight's cabin—an offer she gratefully accepted. "If you need anything, call Mom," he told her as he helped her into Lacy's car. "I'll be there as soon as I can."

"Don't worry about me. Go do your job. I plan to take a nap and be there when you do get in."

"If you're tired, go ahead and go to bed," he said. "I'll just have a bunch of paperwork to deal with." This case had generated more than its fair share of forms and reports.

"Then I'll pour coffee and offer moral support," she said, before waving goodbye and settling back against the seat.

She had the right attitude to be a law enforcement officer's wife, he decided, then went to confer with Travis, who was on the phone with Frank Rizzo. He motioned Dwight to lean in, and together they listened to Rizzo's defense of his sudden departure from the hospital. "Clearly there was nothing I could do for Eddie and there was no sense staying around when there was a shooter on the loose."

"Who hired you to represent Eddie?" Travis asked.

"That information is confidential," Rizzo said.

"I can get a subpoena for not just that information, but anything having to do with Eddie Carstairs," Travis said. "If I have to do that, I promise to take up as much of your and your staff's time as possible. Or you could just answer my question now."

Rizzo's sigh was audible on the phone. "He said he was a friend of the family who wished to remain anonymous. He contacted me by phone—I never saw him, and the number was blocked."

"How did he pay you?"

"With a bank draft made out to my firm, delivered by a private courier within the hour."

"That didn't strike you as odd?" Travis asked.

"No. I deal with any number of very rich and sometimes very eccentric people. I don't question their methods as long as the payment is prompt and in full."

"Has he contacted you about a refund, since your client is dead and won't be needing your services?" Travis asked.

"My fees are nonrefundable."

"Has this man or anyone else contacted you about this?"

"No."

"Let us know if they do," Travis said.

"I don't see how this relates to Mr. Carstairs's death," Rizzo said.

"You don't? You demanded and got bail for Eddie, which put him in a position where the killer could get to him."

Rizzo was silent for a long moment. "I hope you're wrong," he said. "And I have to go now."

The call ended. Travis put away his phone. "Want to bet we'll never hear from him again?" Dwight asked.

"I doubt B or whoever set this up will contact him," Travis said. "They knew when they paid him this case wasn't going to go to trial. They only needed Rizzo to get Eddie released on bail so that they could get a shot at him."

"It had to be a professional hit," Dwight said. "A military sniper couldn't have made a better shot, and the killer didn't leave a shred of evidence."

"Maybe it was a military sniper," Travis said.

"What do you mean?"

Travis shook his head. "I don't know. I'm not ruling anything out right now."

"What's next?" Dwight asked.

"Let's go through Eddie's apartment and try to figure out what he was involved in. So far, B has been very careful. I don't think we're going to find much."

The first item of interest in Eddie's apartment was a box of yellow stationery, a row of cartoon flowers dancing across the bottom of each sheet. "We already knew he sent those threats to Brenda, but it's good to have confirmation," Dwight said.

Dwight flipped through the rest of the contents of the desk in Eddie's bedroom. He pulled a folder from the bottom drawer and looked inside. "Check this out," he said, and handed the folder to Travis.

The sheriff scanned the half dozen photocopies in the folder—all crime scene photos from sheriff's department case files. "Now we know where the photo on that note Eddie sent to Brenda came from," he said.

"That's sick," Dwight said. "It's a good thing you fired him when you did."

The rest of the apartment was full of used furniture, take-out cartons and dirty clothes. Dwight was grateful to leave it and head to his own comfortable home—and the woman waiting for him there.

Brenda smiled up at him when he entered. She was settled on the sofa, her injured arm propped on a pile of pillows. She had dressed and combed her hair and though she was still pale, the tension had faded from her face. Dwight sat beside her. "How are you feeling?" he asked.

"Better," she said. "Much better now." She turned his face toward hers and kissed him, long and hard. Not breaking contact, he slid one arm under her thighs and scooped her onto his lap, being careful not to jostle her injured shoulder.

When they did finally come up for breath, her eyes sparkled. "Tomorrow is my birthday," she said.

"I hadn't forgotten." He tucked a lock of hair behind her ear. "Not a very fun way to spend it."

"I don't know about that. I'm alive. I'm with you. It's funny—before all this happened, I was a little depressed about turning thirty. I felt as if I had reached a milestone in my life and I had nothing to show for it. I don't feel that way anymore."

"Do you think it's because you faced down death and lived?"

"Partly. But I also think it's because I had reached a point where I had lost everything— I was a widow, my job was in jeopardy, my house had burned down, and then my car was wrecked. I had nothing, but instead of all that making me feel defeated, it was incredibly freeing. I had nothing left to lose. I could do anything. I could be with whoever I wanted to be with." She stroked his cheek. "I don't have anywhere to go from here but up."

"As long as you go there with me."

"I've been thinking about my house," she said.

"What about it?"

"I want to rebuild it."

"Sure. We can live wherever you want to live." He would miss the ranch, but there were probably advantages to living in town. And he wanted her to be happy—she deserved that so much.

"I want to stay on the ranch, here with you," she said. "It's beautiful and peaceful here. I love it."

He hoped the relief he felt didn't show on his face. "Then what will you do with the house—rent it out?"

"Something like that. I don't want to build just one house. I want to build a triplex or a fourplex, and make it affordable housing—something Eagle Mountain really needs."

"That sounds like a great idea."

"I'm full of great ideas. I have all kinds of things I want to do at the museum with the money from the Falmont Foundation, and of course, we have a wedding to plan."

"I like the sound of that one. What other ideas do you have?"

"This one." She kissed him again. "And this one." She began unbuttoning his shirt.

"Hey." He wrapped his hand around hers. "You're supposed to be taking it easy. You're recovering from surgery."

"Oh, we can take it easy." She leaned forward and nipped at his jaw. "Slow and easy. Doesn't that sound good?" She leaned back, grinning at him. "Or if you'd rather, you can get a head start on all that paperwork."

"What paperwork?" He hugged her more firmly against him, then leaned over and switched off the lamp, so that the room was lit only by the glow of moonlight through the front windows. Then he pulled her close in a kiss once more. Paperwork could wait—but he didn't have to wait for Brenda anymore.

* * * * *

LET'S TALK

Romance

For exclusive extracts, competitions
and special offers, find us online:

f facebook.com/millsandboon

⊙ @millsandboonuk

🐦 @millsandboon

Or get in touch on 0844 844 1351*

For all the latest titles coming soon,
visit millsandboon.co.uk/nextmonth

*Calls cost 7p per minute plus your phone company's price per
minute access charge